# Finishing Lines

## Hollywood Hopefuls

Jeris Jean

Alpha reader: Michaela Cole

Proofreading by: Michelle K

Cover photography: CJC Photography

❀ Created with Vellum

# Contents

# Prologue

## Wyatt

### One Year Ago

Wyatt wasn't going to cry in front of everyone. He'd already embarrassed himself enough over Sam. He would not do it again. When Sam was on the last verse of the song, Wyatt knew he couldn't hold back the tears any longer, and he started wedging through the crowd in the cafe toward the front door, which was the closest exit. Sam's beautiful voice reverberated through the space, carrying from the mic on the small stage. Wyatt felt it sink into every pore of his skin, battering into his heart. The crowd was thick, full of people filming Sam's performance with their cell phones. It was getting hard to breathe, and Wyatt frantically elbowed past the last few people between him and the door.

He pushed open the door and stumbled onto the sidewalk, disregarding the few smokers congregating near the front window of the cafe. He walked a few paces to the corner and stopped to catch his breath. He leaned against the building's wall, bending over, hands braced on his knees, sucking in the humid night air. At least it was dark. And quiet. He felt the tears slide down his cheeks.

What did it mean? Why had Sam chosen to sing that song? Why had he been looking at Wyatt as he belted every word? And what was the emotion he seemed to be desperately trying to convey with his eyes?

It was too much. Wyatt wanted to scream, and he wanted to curl up into a ball right there on the sidewalk and cry until it didn't hurt so badly. He had never in his life expected something as illogical as love to physically hurt so much. It was unquantifiable, the levels of pain heartbreak could cause a person.

"Wyatt?"

Wyatt heard his name in the distance, but he didn't respond. He couldn't have even if he'd wanted to. His voice didn't work. All he could do was brace himself against that wall and keep breathing as the tears fell.

Footsteps rounded the corner, but Wyatt didn't look up. He stared at the space between his shoes, concentrating on breathing in and out.

"Wyatt." Sam's voice was softer that time. The footsteps halted in front of him, and Sam's Vans came into view, toe-to-toe with his own shoes. "Hey," Sam said gently. "Can you look at me?"

Wyatt didn't respond for a few beats. But he knew what he had to do. Sam didn't move, and he didn't speak again, but Wyatt could feel his stare on him. Wyatt slowly straightened up to standing, eyes still turned down to the sidewalk. He knew his tearstained cheeks would be visible to Sam through the lamplight, so it was no use trying to wipe them. Finally, he raised his eyes to meet Sam's. And he felt his heart squeeze, the pain of it almost causing him to look away. But he didn't. He held Sam's stare.

Sam looked heartbroken, too. His eyes shone with pain and unshed tears, and his youthful features were distorted—his brow was furrowed, his jaw tense. "How can I fix this, Wyatt? What can I say? What can I do?" The desperation in Sam's voice wedged the knife deeper into the open wound in Wyatt's chest.

Wyatt swallowed hard, the possible answers to those questions tearing him apart even further. What could Sam do? Was this even fixable? He'd told Sam that he loved him, and Sam was in love with someone else. He'd told Wyatt he loved him, too, but it wasn't the same way he loved his girlfriend. Wyatt had wanted to disappear after that. He'd wanted to burn out like a star—there one moment and the next simply dust. He didn't want to have that conversation again. But Sam was his best friend. The most important person in his life, apart from his uncle. He couldn't lose him. Even if Sam couldn't love him back the way he wanted, that was the bottom line. He couldn't lose him.

Wyatt was aware that there were people in their periphery, not so subtly trying to catch a glimpse of Sam. Sam ignored them, but Wyatt could feel their eyes on them. Wyatt had known Sam's talent and charisma would bring him fame and attention. And he'd been right. As much as Wyatt hated being observed and judged by strangers, he would have done it for Sam. He could have handled cell phones and catcalls and autograph requests if it meant being at Sam's side. In his life. But at this particular moment, the onlookers just added another layer of humiliation to the devastating scene that was Sam breaking Wyatt's heart—again.

"It's okay," Wyatt finally said, his voice hoarse. "I'll be okay."

Sam's brows drew in closer together, a look of confusion

taking over his face. "What does that mean? What about us? Where do we stand? Because I love you so much, Wyatt. I just..."

Wyatt lifted a hand to halt him. He couldn't go through hearing Sam explain the way their feelings were misaligned again. "I love you too," Wyatt said. "And you're my best friend. We're family now, even." After Wyatt's Uncle Bowen married Sam's older brother Clark, they were officially family. They would always be part of one another's lives. So, Wyatt had to ensure that he could survive it. He needed to be able to be around Sam and have Sam in his life without feeling like his heart was being torn out of his chest every single day. "We're okay, Sam. We're good. I'll get over it."

Sam still looked confused. "What if I don't want you to get over it? What if I want..."

Wyatt lifted a finger to Sam's lips, shushing him. "No," he said. "We're good. Can we please just leave it at that? I don't want to talk about this anymore."

Sam looked like he wanted to argue, so Wyatt shook his head. "Please, Sam. Please let it go." Sam stared into Wyatt's eyes for a long moment, and Wyatt wasn't sure what the emotions swirling in them were. But finally, Sam nodded. Wyatt dropped his finger from Sam's lips and used every ounce of energy and fortitude he possessed to fake a small smile.

Sam frowned. "But you're okay? You're not mad at me?"

"I'm not mad at you," Wyatt assured him. And it was the truth. He wasn't mad at Sam. He was just devastated that the man he loved was never going to be his the way he wanted him. But that would have to be okay. Because having Sam in his life was essential, and Wyatt would do whatever he needed to in order to make it bearable.

# Chapter One

## Sam

"Come on, Dan-o, we have plenty of time before the flight. It's one quick stop." Sam aimed for light and breezy with his tone, but even he could hear the tinges of whining at the edges. He slid into the passenger seat of the sedan, refusing to ride in the backseat despite the protests of his personal security guard, Dan Banks. They'd had the "the backseat is safer and less visible" conversation more than a few times, and despite Dan being built like a tank and intimidating to just about everyone, Sam had weaseled his way into the front seat with a dimpled grin and the characteristic charm that had shot him to the top of the Hollywood A-list over the past year.

"No." Dan's reply was calm yet firm as he fastened his seat belt and lowered his Ray-Bans into place.

"But why not? We don't need to be three hours early for the flight. Remember how annoying it is to keep people away from me at the airport? You hate the airport. The less time there, the better," Sam said, as if it was all settled. He slid his own shades on and paired his phone to the car, quickly starting his "Vail, Baby!" playlist that he'd specifically made for this trip. *One did not simply travel to his brother's destination wedding in the mountains without the proper tunes.*

Dan pulled the sedan out of the secure parking garage of Sam's apartment complex, and Sam knew his eagle eyes were surveying every other car and pedestrian in the vicinity, watching for paparazzi or other potential threats. The work of the personal security for Sam Deerwood, the star of the hit TV series *Ominous* and Hollywood's favorite "It boy" was never-ending. But Dan was the best, and Sam paid him the big bucks to keep him safe. "Actually," Dan said as they made their way toward the highway, "I don't hate the airport. I hate you stopping to take selfies and sign autographs at the airport. It's not a secure environment in which to do so."

"I can't be a dick, though," Sam replied immediately. "My fans are important to me."

"And keeping you safe is important to me."

"I am safe at the cafe, though," Sam argued. "We can go in the back entrance. Come on, Big Dan. Five minutes."

Dan didn't respond immediately. He simply wove through the cars with ease, making his way down the highway.

"Please," Sam said, his voice earnest. He knew he could be a little bit of a shit to deal with, but this was important to him. And in their seven months working together, Dan had grown to know Sam pretty well. He knew when he was being serious, and he seemed to have a big-brotherly soft spot for the younger man.

Dan let out a put-upon sigh and changed lanes, making for the exit for the cafe. Sam grinned. "Thank you, Dan-the-Man. I owe you one."

"You owe me more than one, kid." Dan's lips twitched

the slightest bit before settling back into the hard line they usually held. "And quit it with the stupid nicknames, would you? We've been over this."

"I'm so sorry, Daniel, sir."

Dan mumbled something Sam couldn't quite hear.

"What was that?" Sam had one red brow raised in curiosity.

"I said my name's not Daniel either," Dan said.

"Wait," Sam said, chuckling a bit. He lifted his sunglasses to his forehead to better assess Dan's profile as they spoke. "Dan's not short for anything? It's just 'Dan'? Are your parents complete weirdos or what? Who does that?"

"Worse," Dan said. He had turned onto the cafe's street, moving slowly. Sam couldn't see his eyes behind his shades, but he was certain Dan was assessing their surroundings. If it was too crowded or any paparazzi were parked out front of the cafe, Dan might still call this little field trip off.

"What do you mean?" Sam asked. "What's worse than people naming their child 'Dan-not-short-for-Daniel'?"

Dan sighed again. "My mom was a big *Cheers* fan."

Sam's eyes widened and sparkled. "No way...they named you..."

"Danson," Dan said, nodding. "My mom really had the hots for Sam Malone."

"Your name is Danson. After Ted Danson?"

"Yup."

Sam cackled, and Dan's lips twitched in amusement. "I'm sorry," Sam said through fits of giggles. "That is the best thing I've heard in a long, long time, Big Dan."

"Damn it," Dan said. "I told you my real name so you'd quit it with the dumbass nicknames."

"Oh, I am far from done," Sam said, a wicked glint in his

eye. "You've just given me endless new material. Like...
wait..." It took Sam a second to rein in his laughter again.
"We're going to the cafe...where everybody knows your
name!" Sam's shoulders shook as he amused himself with
his own jokes.

Dan groaned as he pulled into the alley behind the cafe.
"That's enough now," Dan said when he put the car into
park. "I was nice enough to make this detour for you."

"You're right," Sam said, wiping the tears of laughter
from his eyes. "Thank you," he added.

Dan got out of the vehicle first, and Sam knew to wait
until he gave the all clear before exiting the car. Dan went
up to the back door of the cafe and entered using the pass-
code at the door's entrance. It wasn't standard to have a
coded entrance to a cafe from the alley, but due to Sam's
celebrity status, all of Sam's siblings had had to make some
changes in their lives, including at their places of business.
Part of Sam felt guilty about making their lives more
complicated, but they'd never once made him feel anything
other than their love for and pride in him. So, he didn't
worry about it too much. As much as Sam had dreamed of
this level of fame, he'd been naive when it came to the toll
his being easily recognized would take on those close to
him. Dan disappeared into the cafe and then reappeared at
Sam's door, pulling it open for him. "All good," he said.

Sam exited the car, the nerves starting to hit. He hadn't
really expected Dan to be willing to swing by the cafe. And
now that they were here, he had no idea what he was going
to say or do. He came to see Wyatt, of course. No matter
what their relationship was in technical terms, Wyatt was
still the most important person in Sam's world. And he just
wanted to see his face. He'd also thought it would be wise to
check in with him before the big wedding week

commenced. They'd be spending a lot of time together over the next week, and he wanted to make sure Wyatt was feeling okay with that. And if there was anything Sam could do to make it easier. And maybe to tell Wyatt how much he loved him and wanted them to be together. *Wait. No. Not that last one.* They'd settled that last year. Wyatt didn't want to be with him that way. And they were family now. They were friends. That was the deal. That was the plan. And Sam could respect that. But just because they couldn't be together didn't mean he didn't still harbor feelings for Wyatt. He had a suspicion that was something he'd do for the rest of his life.

Sam entered the cafe, Dan right behind him. It was quiet and dimly lit. This time of morning, before they opened, Sam's brother Matt, who owned the cafe, was usually stocking the pastries for the day with his business partner, Bowen, who was also Wyatt's uncle. Because Sam's brother and Wyatt's uncle worked together, and because Bowen had married Sam's other brother, Clark, Wyatt and Sam were part of one another's lives. No matter what was going on between the two of them. Wyatt often joined Matt and Bowen in the early morning pastry ritual, as he was their business manager and often used the time when they filled the cases with Danishes and muffins to give them a brief overview of how the cafe was doing and addressed any other business-related stuff that needed discussing.

Sam could hear Blink 182's "I Miss You" softly playing from a speaker up front as he made his way through the kitchen of the cafe and pushed the swinging door open.

"Shit!" A blue-haired woman holding a box of pastries turned to face Sam, eyes wide. "You scared me, Sam!"

"Sorry, Jade," Sam said, giving her an apologetic smile. "Didn't Darlin' Dan here warn you I was coming?"

They both turned to Dan, who was peering through the front windows of the cafe, no doubt on the lookout for any potential threats.

"No, he did not," she said, shaking her head as she set the pastry box on the top of the counter. "What can I do for you?" She was friendly and not at all impressed with Sam's celebrity status, having worked for Matt and Bowen since before Sam had had his big break.

Sam couldn't help his eyes darting around the space, his heart falling when he didn't see anyone else around. "I was looking for Wyatt," he said. "I thought he stocked the morning pastries."

Jade nodded, adjusting the ties of her apron. "He normally does, but the whole crew left for the airport," she said, squinting an eye at Sam. "Shouldn't you be doing the same?"

"Yes," Dan's deep voice said from the other side of the counter.

Disappointment hit Sam hard, but he didn't want to let on too much. "I just figured I might catch him here first where it would be quiet," Sam said, shrugging. "No privacy at the airport."

"Don't they have fancy special lounges for VIPs like you?" Jade said, punching his arm playfully.

"They do," Sam said. "But my annoying-ass family will all be crowded in there, too." He smiled, knowing that Jade was well aware that he was kidding and that he loved his siblings dearly.

"Sorry," Jade said, finally. "Want a pastry for the road?" She gestured to the half-full box atop the counter.

Sam shook his head. "Nah, thanks though."

"What about you, Danson?" she asked.

Sam's eyes widened before he hit Dan with a vicious glare. "Jade knew your real name before I did?"

Dan cracked a tiny smile. "She asked," he said simply, reaching out to accept a glazed donut from the box Jade had since shoved in his direction.

"Unbelievable," Sam said, shaking his head. "But thanks, Jade," he added, giving her a small wave. "I guess I have a plane to catch." He hoped he didn't sound too dejected and pathetic at having missed Wyatt.

"Have fun this week!" Jade called. "I want pics. You tell Bowen he's on mopping duty for a month if he doesn't keep me posted."

"Will do," Sam called back.

He and Dan returned to the sedan, Sam sinking into his seat with a long sigh.

"Sorry," Dan said gruffly as he pulled the car back down the alley. "I didn't realize why you wanted to stop."

"It's okay," Sam said, trying his best to believe that.

* * *

They'd made it through security with nothing more than a few curious glances, which was a miracle in Sam's world these days. A couple of people eyed him suspiciously, with the classic "Do I know you from somewhere?" squint, but either they couldn't place him, or they weren't fans. While Sam was recognizable with his tousled red hair and boyish good looks, he was mostly popular with teens. And their parents. He was big with the cougar crowd, if the amount of moms he'd been asked to pose for selfies with was any indication. He thought it was a trip, and most of the time he didn't mind the attention one bit. The only time it grated was when it made it difficult for him to go about his daily life or if it impacted his loved ones.

"That wasn't so bad," Sam said to Dan. "Told you we didn't need to be here four hours early."

Dan swiped Sam's carry-on bag from him, tossing his own bag atop it, looping the bag's strap over the carry-on bag's extended handle. Sam had long since given up arguing with Dan about pulling his own luggage. The big guy was not having it. Apparently, it made Sam "too slow" when he carried his own bag.

"Just focus on moving your ass," Dan said as he herded Sam toward their airline's first-class lounge. "Don't get cocky yet." Dan set a swift pace with his long strides, eyes flitting around, missing nothing. "The less time we're in the open, the better."

Sam was about to tease Dan, mainly in an attempt to distract himself from his stupid disappointment about missing Wyatt, but a high-pitched squeal stopped him. He felt the hairs on his arms raise and a flush hit him hard at the now-familiar sound. Dan's body tensed beside him, and he stepped between Sam and the teen, who was bouncing on their feet and flapping their hands in excitement.

"It's Sam Deerwood! From *Ominous*! Amy!"

"Holy shit!" Another teen turned toward Sam and lifted her hands to her face.

The two teens' dramatics had caused other passersby to stop and look around, and soon people were circled around them, blocking them from advancing any further. Dan had his hands up, body shielding Sam as much as possible, and he was telling the gathering crowd to stay back. The crowd was firing questions at Sam a mile a minute as Dan looked at Sam over his shoulder. "Call Clark," Dan ordered, his voice deep and loud to cut through the clamoring crowd.

"Can I get a selfie?"

"Will you sign this for me?"

"Caspian! I love you!"

"Sam! Where's Blair?"

"Is Caspian's dad coming back from the dead?"

"Where are you going?"

"Just one picture?"

"My sister loves you."

"He's not taking photos," Dan said. "He has a plane to catch."

The crowd wielded their cell phones, no doubt filming and snapping photos, straining for any glimpse of Sam they could manage. Sam felt bad hiding behind Dan, but he knew it wasn't safe for him in an uncontrolled group like this. He'd learned that the hard way. That was why he'd hired Dan in the first place.

Sam managed to get his phone out of his pocket and dial Clark. His middle brother was protective as a bulldog, and he had helped Dan more than once when one bodyguard wasn't enough. Clark had actually pushed for Sam to get a larger security detail, which Sam had dismissed immediately. He wasn't freaking Harry Styles, for God's sake. But at that particular moment, Sam started to see the merit in Clark's suggestion. The crowd was pushing closer, despite Dan's stern orders to give him space. Sam trembled, not knowing what to do. If he gave them what they wanted, he'd be here all day. But if he was an asshole, it was bad for his image. He never knew how to handle these situations, and he had honestly been in denial that he needed a better plan. It was hard to believe that people would react this way to him. A year ago, he was a nobody. And now he had people trying to push past 280 pounds of angry muscle to get a pic of him.

The phone at Sam's ear rang, and he covered his other ear with his free hand, ducking and facing the wall to hear Clark.

"Hello?" Clark's voice immediately brought a drop of calm to Sam's system.

"We got cornered in the concourse," Sam said. "Between security and the lounge."

"Okay. We're here. I'll get some security officers and be there in a second."

"Thanks," Sam said, relieved that his brother was on the way.

In less than two minutes, armed security officers came marching down the concourse, parting the crowd and barking at them to disperse. Sam felt his heart rate slow a fraction when there was some space around them. Dan was right by his side, and behind the security officers that had broken up the crowd was his brother Clark. Sam was immediately filled with relief at the sight of his big brother. Nothing and no one was getting through Clark.

Clark gave Sam a quick once-over, searching for any sign of distress. As the security guards shooed away the crowd, Clark's serious eyes met Sam's. "You okay?" he asked.

Sam swallowed hard and nodded. "I am now."

The security guards led the way, escorting them to their lounge, Dan and Clark flanking Sam protectively. While Clark asked Dan what happened, Sam worked on calming his galloping heart.

# Chapter Two

## Wyatt

"How long is this trail again?" Bowen tried to keep his voice nonchalant, but the words came out in short bursts of what might have been described as breathless gasps.

Wyatt slowed his pace a bit to allow his uncle to keep stride with him. "Don't worry," Wyatt said, not sounding winded in the least. "We're only doing a third of the trail. Just to the other side of the village and back."

"A third of how far, though?" Bowen said, giving his nephew side-eye. "Not all of us are twenty-four, you know. And..." Bowen's pace slowed as the trail merged with a wide sidewalk of the downtown Vail streets. He sucked in a deep breath then finished his sentence, "The altitude." Wyatt slowed too, amused at his uncle's sweat-soaked, clearly out-of-shape state. "I'm not used to it," Bowen added. He slowly staggered to a stop at an intersection, placing his hands on his knees and pulling in deep breaths.

"Marriage has made you soft, Uncle Bo," Wyatt said, smiling at him.

"Oh no," Bowen said, standing tall and shooting Wyatt

a wicked grin. "I'll assure you there is nothing soft about me when it comes to my marriage."

Wyatt rolled his eyes. "Don't be gross."

The walk sign lit up, and Bowen groaned as they started up again, this time at a slow jog.

"Remind me why I'm running up a mountain on my vacation," Bowen grumbled.

"First, you are hardly running up the mountain," Wyatt said. "And you offered to run with me. If I'm going to do a half-marathon, I can't take a week off of training. Wedding week or not."

They found a rhythm, which was much slower than Wyatt would have set had he been running alone, but he appreciated the company.

They'd landed in Vail earlier that morning, and Wyatt and Bowen were among the first to arrive at the massive lodge their group had rented out for the week. Wyatt had taken the early arrival as an opportunity to claim his room at the house, but once he'd done that, he felt overwhelmed with nervous energy. Truth be told, he was equal parts anxious and excited to see Sam. It had been several months —at least three—since Wyatt and Sam had been face-to-face. And the thought of seeing him had Wyatt's skin feeling too tight and his body too restless.

After basically just dropping his luggage in a room, Wyatt had said he was going to take a run, and Bowen had offered to go with him, leaving his husband, Clark, back at the house where he was going over wedding details with one of the grooms, Matt. Matt was Clark's brother and Bowen's business partner, and he was finally getting married to his longtime fiancé, Jasper.

Matt and Jasper's wedding was going to be a modestly sized, yet lavish affair. Jasper was a television executive with several huge hits to his credit, and Matt was a quasi celebrity in his own right, having gone viral on social media as "hot coffee guy" back when he was a barista on the film lot where he met Jasper. Throw in the fact that Matt's younger brother was Sam Deerwood, Hollywood-heart-throb-of-the-moment, and their wedding was kind of a big deal. Wyatt knew that part of the reason they'd chosen to have their wedding in Vail rather than LA was to avoid any paparazzi or media attention so that Sam could attend in peace. Several of Jasper's closest friends were also famous, so add that to the fact that he and Matt had a home in the Colorado mountains that was a beloved getaway for them, and Vail was the perfect destination.

The town was lovely in early fall. It looked like something out of a fairy tale, even when it wasn't peak season for tourists. Come winter, the place would be swamped with out-of-town skiers and snowboarders flocking to the beautiful Colorado mountains for their cold-weather getaways. But now, in September, the leaves were starting to change, the flowers were still in bloom at the base of the mountains, and they were able to host a wedding full of high-profile guests in semiprivacy. The wide cobblestone streets were lined with charming ski village shops and restaurants. Hundreds of massive hanging baskets with flowers spilling out of them hung along sidewalks. The whole town was nestled in below the majestic mountains keeping watch over the quaint village. Despite the altitude, which did require some getting used to, Wyatt thought the place was perfect. There were endless trails of various lengths and elevations. The views were stunning. And, best of all, he hadn't seen a single paparazzo since they'd touched down in Denver.

Wyatt slowed in front of a coffee shop, and Bowen huffed out an "Oh thank God."

Wyatt grinned at his uncle, who, Wyatt had to admit, was in excellent shape for nearly forty. He was just being a drama queen about being winded. They went into the coffee shop, and five minutes later they were seated with tall ice waters and a pair of buttery croissants. Bowen took a large bite, moaning obscenely as he chewed.

"Must you?" Wyatt's eyes darted around the sparsely filled room. His uncle was notorious for making his appreciation of food sound downright pornographic. That, too, Wyatt was certain, was mostly an act for attention. His uncle Bowen was nothing if not one to make his presence known.

Bowen closed his eyes as he slowly swallowed his bite of pastry. Wyatt glared at him as he took his time savoring every last bit. "I must," Bowen said finally, flashing a toothy grin at Wyatt. "You made me run, and now I will sit and enjoy my reward to my heart's content. And no one can stop me, least of all you, mister." He winked at Wyatt.

Wyatt rolled his eyes and bit into his own croissant, which was, in fact, delicious.

"I think I've worked out what I'm going to say," Bowen told Wyatt as they ate.

"What do you mean?" Wyatt furrowed his brow.

"For the ceremony," Bowen said.

"Why would you say anything?"

"Because I'm the officiant, of course," Bowen said, as if that sentence made any sense in any universe.

"You're the what now?"

"The officiant. Matt and Jasper asked me to do it. I am an ordained officiant, you know."

Wyatt sighed. He hadn't known that. But there wasn't much his uncle could say that would surprise him anymore.

"They asked you to officiate the wedding," Wyatt repeated, "and you're just now thinking up what you're going to say?"

"I have five days," Bowen said, flapping his hand in front of his face like that was the most insignificant detail he'd ever been bothered with in his life.

"I suppose there's like a...script...of some kind, yes?" Wyatt was prone to worrying. And rule and regulation following. He was a numbers guy. A by-the-book guy.

"Yes," Bowen said. "There are suggested scripts out there. But you know me. I like to go off-book."

"You realize that their wedding isn't about you giving a performance, right?"

"Settle down, killer," Bowen said to Wyatt with a chuckle. "It's all under control. Nothing for you to worry about."

Wyatt nodded, accepting that this didn't actually have anything to do with him and wasn't something he'd need to micromanage.

"Speaking of worries," Bowen said, his voice sounding more serious. "Are you nervous about Sam?"

Wyatt's insides heated and flipped at the mention of Sam's name. Like they always did. But he didn't show an outward reaction. He never did. "Why would I be worried?" His words sounded fairly even, and if he'd been speaking to anyone other than his uncle, who had raised him since he was twelve, he would have gotten away with it.

"When's the last time the two of you spent any real time together?" Bowen's words were soft, not accusatory. It was clear he was just looking out for Wyatt. But this was the last thing Wyatt wanted to think about, let alone discuss. Hell, he'd gone for the run with the sole purpose of avoiding the fact that Sam would be arriving at the lodge any time now.

"It's been a while," Wyatt said. The truth was, Wyatt

had twisted and bent his schedule a million ways from Sunday to avoid crossing paths with Sam. It had been too painful, especially when Wyatt had heard Sam had broken up with his girlfriend again and was once again on the market. It would have been too hard to have Sam right there, unattached, and still not letting Wyatt love him.

"And how do you feel about that?" Bowen was prodding, but Wyatt knew it was out of concern.

"I feel like I don't want anyone to make a big deal out of it," he said, sounding a bit snappier than he'd intended. Bowen stared at him, studying him in a way that told Wyatt he could see right through him.

"Okay," Bowen said finally. "But if you need to...go for a run or anything, I'm here, okay?"

"Thanks," Wyatt said softly.

"I love you, kiddo," Bowen said. "Even if you do have a man bun now."

Wyatt ran his hands over his sweat-damp, grown-out locks, which were pulled back into the man bun in question. "Hey, I thought you said it looked good?"

Bowen barked out a laugh. "It does. But I'm still going to give you shit." He winked at his nephew.

"You're just jealous that all the hair you can grow now is on your back," Wyatt said, shooting an impish grin at Bowen.

"I told you that in confidence! You're my assistant. Who else is supposed to book my waxing appointments? You can't use that employer/employee confidential information to roast me."

"Actually, I can, and I will. It's in my contract."

Bowen's eyes widened. "Is it really?"

Wyatt laughed. "No. But it's good to know I could literally put anything in my contract, and you'd have no idea. Looks like I'm getting a raise."

Bowen balled up his napkin and pelted Wyatt in the nose with it. They both laughed and enjoyed their little moment in the coffee shop. The calm before the storm, so to speak.

"You think anyone will be at the house when we get back?" Wyatt's question was supposed to sound like general curiosity, but he knew that Bowen was on to him, especially since they'd just talked about Sam. The lodge Jasper and Matt had rented out for the wedding week was massive. Apparently, since a few of the guests had personal security teams, they'd insisted on keeping everyone in one location that they could closely monitor. It still baffled Wyatt that anyone he knew was that level of famous. The most famous among them at the moment was his former best friend. It was surreal to say the least.

"I imagine so," Bowen said, looking at his watch. We've been gone a couple of hours now."

Wyatt nodded. "Glad we claimed our rooms first," he said.

"Matt won't put you in the same room with Sam, if that's what you're worried about," Bowen assured him. "He knows things are...complicated with you two. We are all aware," Bowen said.

"Great." Wyatt sighed, fiddling with his water cup. "Like we're two troublemaking kids who can't have their desks beside one another?"

"No," Bowen said. "Like you're two people we love very much and don't want to be uncomfortable in any way if we can avoid it."

Wyatt bit his lip and nodded. His found family was pretty amazing that way. As awkward as it was that he and

Sam were part of the same family now, through marriage and business ties, no one had ever made Wyatt feel like they were choosing sides. Even Sam's siblings had shown Wyatt nothing but friendship and kindness.

Maybe he didn't really have anything to worry about. It was a few days that he and Sam would be together. In a massive lodge with tons of other guests. It wouldn't be that awkward. Maybe it wouldn't be awkward at all. Probably nothing to worry about.

# Chapter Three

## Sam

Sam's jaw dropped when they pulled up to the rental house. "House" probably wasn't the correct word. It was more like a mountainside mansion. The enormous stone and wood exterior blended into the surrounding landscape, the sky-high peaks of the roofline mimicking the surrounding mountains.

Dan put the car in park near the front entrance and was around the hood and opening Sam's door before Sam could slide his feet back into the Jordans he'd slipped off on the ride up from the airport.

Sam stepped out and inhaled deeply. "The mountains smell different, don't they, Daniel Tiger?" He stretched his lanky arms out wide and slowly turned in a circle, absorbing the beauty of the view.

Dan grunted something vaguely affirmative as he pocketed the car keys and began scanning the perimeter of the property. "You go inside. I'm going to take a quick look around."

"What?" Sam said, mock shock in his voice. "You don't want to clear the house before I step in? Is my safety no longer paramount among your concerns? I'm hurt, Big Guy."

"Wilkinson is already inside," Dan said, nodding to the Apple Watch on his wrist.

"Wilkinson?" Sam whined. "I didn't know you were bringing Mean Keanu." Sam was generally familiar with the other guys that worked with Dan at Hicks-Olson, the security agency. Sam had partially selected Hicks-Olson on the recommendation of Jasper, his soon-to-be brother-in-law, who knew the agency served some of Jasper's high-profile friends, but also because he could call it the HO agency. Yes, Sam might be a millionaire now, but he was still a child when it came to his sense of humor.

"He's good at his job. So what if he's not personable?" Dan started ushering Sam up the stone pathway toward the front door. "Besides, with three of you under the same roof, we need all the hands on deck we can get."

"Three of us?"

Dan didn't have time to respond before the front door flung open, and a tattooed arm reached out and pulled Sam into the house. "Thank fuck," Matt said, tugging his brother through the entryway and into the house proper, not allowing time for introductions or so much as a "hello" to Dan, who'd shut the door behind them, presumably to do his "perimeter check" of the property.

"What's happening?" Sam said, staggering along behind his big brother.

"Groom problems," Matt said, not bothering to let go of Sam's shirt as he dragged him into an enormous, open great room. The vaulted ceilings made the place feel almost roofless. To the right, there was a sitting room with a stone fireplace that reached no less than twenty feet tall, extending all the way to the peak of the ceiling. To the left, there was a massive kitchen with an island the size of a twin bed. The far wall of the entire house was windows. The mountains stood tall in the distance; the purpling sky offset by the dusky, snow-peaked ridges.

Just off the kitchen, Matt finally halted in front of a massive, twelve-seater dining table. The top was littered with what looked like...yard waste? Pinecones and sprigs of spruce and various different leaves and flora littered the surface. Matt dropped Sam's shirt from his fist and ran his hands through his platinum-blond hair, a style choice he'd made specially for the wedding. Matt was a fan of changing his hair color frequently, but platinum was his fiancé's favorite, so he'd stripped away the color.

"What am I looking at, Matty?"

Matt extended one tattooed arm at the mess in front of them. "The fucking boutonnieres, apparently." His tone was a bit panicked, and when he stopped to finally look at Sam, Sam could see the tension in his face.

His brother had always been the one to calm everyone else down when they were freaking out. When Sam had run out of gas on the interstate, Matt had been the one to come rescue him and sort it out. When Mara had screwed up the paperwork for her dorm at UCLA, Matt had calmly instructed her to look up the university housing office's number and give them a call. And when Clark and Bowen had up and eloped in Las Vegas one weekend, Matt had been the one covering for them back home at the cafe. He was everyone's rock. And now, he needed someone to be there for him. Helping him with his pre-wedding anxiety was the least Sam could do for him.

"Where's Clark?" Sam asked, hoping that there'd be other reinforcements. He knew Clark had arrived at the Denver airport when he and Dan had, but then Dan had gotten into a debate with the car rental desk about some of the fine print in the contract. Sam had been genuinely shocked to learn that anyone read those. But, as it were, Dan did. So even if they'd been on the same flight, Sam and Dan would have been behind him.

"I sent him to meet the caterer," Matt said. "Apparently there was some confusion about the vegan cake. I don't know." Matt ran a hand over his face. "I just couldn't deal with it, so I sent Clark. He knows how to get shit done."

Sam nodded. "That he does."

"But now I'm stuck here with this," Matt said, gesturing to the chaos on the top of the dining table.

Sam put his hands on his hips and surveyed the assortment of boutonniere accoutrement. "Lucky for you," he said, drawing on his acting experience to fake confidence he absolutely didn't feel, "I am great with floral design."

Matt's shoulders immediately relaxed as he sighed in relief. Apparently, he was so frazzled he was willing to believe the ridiculous statement. Sam slowly paced the length of the table, occasionally reaching out to touch an aspen leaf or a sprig of spruce. There was a box in the center of the table with twine, wire cutters, coils of thin green wire, and what looked to Sam like rolls of green Washi tape. "Oh, I can work with this," Sam assured Matt. He still had absolutely no idea what to do with any of it, but Matt had stopped vibrating with anxiety, so he would keep up the charade. "Can I ask," Sam said carefully, picking up some berries and examining them, "why you opted for the DIY boutonniere kit? Don't they have proper florists in Colorado?"

Matt pulled one of the massive wooden chairs out from the table and slumped into it. "That was my fault," he said, sliding some of the supplies into a heap to make room to prop up an elbow and resting his chin in his hand, like he was trying to solve a puzzle. "I was in charge of ordering them, and when I looked online, you could either get them for twenty dollars apiece or fifteen dollars apiece. Even I can do the math on that savings. We needed ten, so I thought I'd save us fifty dollars. I just assumed that they'd have one less ribbon or leaf or something. Turns out I simply ordered the florals needed. Not the assembly or labor." He shook his head miserably. "Apparently, lots of brides and grooms like to DIY things these days. Who knew?"

"You do know you're marrying a millionaire, right? I think you could have swung the extra fifty dollars." Sam smiled at his brother.

"I'm still not used to it," Matt said with a rueful expression on his face.

"I get that," Sam said, nodding. "Me, either."

The Deerwoods had grown up poor. They'd struggled to survive, really, for years. Matt had worked insane hours as a barista to keep his siblings fed and clothed, and it wasn't until recently that they'd found themselves in drastically different circumstances. Matt was a successful business owner in his own right, and he was marrying a millionaire television executive. And Sam's most recent *Ominous* contract had him making $30,000 an episode. He could hardly believe it. He still couldn't quite conceive of just how much money that was. And he certainly understood why Matt was still in the habit of cutting costs where he could. Spending money wasn't something you just immediately felt comfortable doing when you'd spent most of your life scrounging.

Sam pulled out a chair and sat beside Matt. "Okay," Sam said. "We need ten of these bad boys. So that means we should figure out what will go into each of the ten. Like..." He picked up a sprig of spruce. "It looks like these are the biggest pieces. So maybe one of these per boutonniere?"

Matt nodded. "Yeah," he said. "That makes sense. And then a leaf and a berry?"

"That's overkill, dude," Sam said. "Looks like some of them will be spruce and berry, and some will be aspen and pinecone?"

Footsteps sounded behind them, and Sam looked over his shoulder to see Dan walk in. He eyed Matt and Sam and the table full of floral arranging supplies. "What do we have here?" He was good at keeping his voice even, but there was a slight smirk on the big guy's face.

"Boutonnieres," Sam said cheerfully. "Pull up a seat, Dan Ackroyd. You're on floral tape duty."

It turned out that there really was a how-to for anything on YouTube these days. After a handful of hideous, dilapidated attempts, Sam, Matt, and Dan had all but perfected the art of boutonniere design. Or at least they could make something passably boutonniere-esque that didn't fall apart at the slightest touch, and that was a win.

"So do you know the room situation?" Sam asked Matt. "You didn't exactly give me the tour when I got here." He gave his brother a pointed look before wrapping the green wire around a spruce stem.

"I kind of figured I'd leave it up to Dan and the guys," Matt said. "Jasper and I have the master, of course," he said. "The security team will probably want to put you, Grayson, and Finn in the basement or something. Fewer windows." Matt winked at Sam. From what Sam had seen, there was no room in the lodge without enormous windows. And they were far enough away from any traffic or passersby that it probably didn't matter what room he or the other celebrity guests were in. Jasper was more than familiar with planning around the needs of his famous employees and friends. He no doubt selected the most secluded lodge in all of Vail.

"So...do we have to share rooms at all? Or do I get my own?" Sam asked the question casually, though he suspected Matt could tell he was fishing.

"You're not rooming with Wyatt, if that's what you're asking," Matt said. "There will be no drama on my wedding week, Sam. None."

"I didn't say anything about Wyatt," Sam said defensively. "I was just curious where I'm sleeping while I'm here. Is that a crime?"

"I mean it, Sam," Matt said. "I know it's going to be hard for you to be around Wyatt this week, but I need you to make it work, okay?"

Sam felt a knot form in his gut. Of course he wanted to make this week drama free for Matt. He didn't want drama either. But there was no way he could be around Wyatt without it affecting him. It was impossible.

"I promise," Sam said. "It won't be a big deal at all."

"What won't be a big deal at all?"

The deep voice that had asked the question belonged to Bowen, who strolled into the dining room in running clothes, a half-empty bottle of water in his hand.

"Nothing," Sam said quickly, giving Bowen a smile in greeting. "We were just..."

Sam didn't finish his sentence. His mouth forgot how to speak. His lungs seemed to forget how to breathe. And all his eyes could do was stare at the man who'd just walked in.

Wyatt.

Wyatt looked different, and Sam hungrily took in every change—from the fact that his dark hair was long enough to be pulled back off his face, to the way that his arms looked lean and more defined than Sam remembered them. Sam's entire body felt flushed at the sight of him, and the knot in his stomach flipped. Wyatt wore sweats and a T-shirt, and he looked extremely fit. Since when did Wyatt wear sweats? Where was his button-down and the cell phone he'd always had glued to his hand? He'd changed so much. Had it really been that long since he'd seen Wyatt face-to-face? He tried to do the math. It had been over a couple of months. Maybe three or four? Far too long. What else was different about Wyatt? Did he have a whole new life now that Sam knew nothing about? A life where he had long hair and wore sweats and looked hotter than was fair for a human to look?

Wyatt's hazel eyes locked on Sam's, and Sam's head spun.

"Hi," Wyatt said, his mouth curving into a tentative smile.

"Hi," Sam managed.

The air between them was charged, and Sam had lost all concept of other things even existing. The room was gone, the tables, Dan and Matt and Bowen; it was all just him and Wyatt, and the aching in his chest. Silence rode the vibrating energy between them, until Sam could no longer take it.

"I make boutonnieres now," he said, brandishing his latest creation.

Wyatt's eyes crinkled and a grin spread across his face. "Your talents never cease to amaze," he said. And Sam felt his entire body tingle in happiness at the sight.

# Chapter Four

## Wyatt

All things considered, Wyatt was handling his emotions well. He'd had a slight slip when he felt his face light up when Sam had smiled at him while holding up the world's derpiest boutonniere. But he'd quickly regained his composure. He'd excused himself from the floral sprig forest that was the dining room to take a shower. The time under the hot water helped him recalibrate after the knock his equilibrium had taken at the sight of Sam's adorable, freckled smile.

Wyatt massaged shampoo into his scalp thoroughly, replaying the rollercoaster of feelings he'd been through already that day. First there had been the nerves about traveling and seeing Sam again. He'd thought the run and his chat with Bowen would clear his mind and bring him back to the headspace he'd need to get through this week, but seeing Sam sitting at that table, smiling at him like that...It had been enough to make Wyatt want to forget he was a composed adult and throw his arms around Sam and squeeze until the last year was erased and nothing was damaged between them. Wyatt rinsed his hair and focused on his mantra for the week. *Be present. Be supportive of Matt and Jasper. This is not about you and Sam.*

Wyatt took a minute to survey the dials on the wall of the enormous, fancy shower he was in, trying to remember how to turn the water on and off. He'd not paid close attention to what he was doing when he'd gotten into the shower. He'd been too focused on breathing and calming down. He turned the dial that seemed most logical, and the water shut off. He grabbed the fluffy white towel he'd hung on the hook outside the shower and dried off efficiently. His longer hair did take a bit to dry, but he squeezed out as much water as he could with the towel before wrapping it around his waist.

When he stepped out of the bathroom, which was an en suite for the bedroom he'd claimed earlier, he startled when he realized he wasn't alone. On the king bed, right beside his open suitcase, sat Sam. He was cross-legged and looking at something on his phone. Wyatt clutched his towel tightly at his waist and went straight for the suitcase, hoping to grab some clothes without descending into a complete meltdown at the situation. Sam was here, on his bed, and Wyatt wasn't wearing any clothes. Wyatt's brain whirred, and his skin flushed, and his dick stirred at the sight of Sam's messy red locks falling into his eyes and his lanky body curled up cozily on the bed like it was the most normal thing in the world.

Wyatt cleared his throat, and Sam looked up. His eyes widened and ran up and down Wyatt's damp, towel-clad body. Wyatt saw Sam's Adam's apple bob as he swallowed, and then a tentative smile curved his lips. "Uh...hey," Sam said. "Sorry. I can let you get dressed." He slid toward the side of the bed as if to disembark.

"No, it's fine," Wyatt heard himself say. "What's up?" Wyatt had no clue how he was managing to sound so nonchalant, but he was pleased to hear the Tilt-A-Whirl of feelings in his brain wasn't apparent in his voice. He went to the suitcase, keeping his eyes fixed on the clothing he was grabbing rather than Sam.

"Okay," Sam said, still getting off the bed and standing on the opposite side of it from Wyatt. "I just thought we could...you know...talk? Clear the air a bit?"

Wyatt forced himself not to react. He carefully piled the pants, shirt, socks, and underwear he'd planned to wear that evening neatly onto the bed as he waited for Sam to speak, which he didn't immediately do. Wyatt fought the urge to look at Sam, but he knew he couldn't. He was using all the strength he possessed to remain composed. He heard Sam let out a long breath. "You look so different," he said finally.

Wyatt looked up then to see Sam studying him. Wyatt hated his stupid body for flushing at Sam's perusal. His heart thumped and his cheeks flamed, and he instinctively tightened his abs, which he immediately tried to relax, but then he realized Sam might notice him flexing and unflexing, and that would be even more awkward than just flexing, so he held them in as casually as he could.

"I started running," Wyatt said, shrugging a shoulder. "It's supposed to help with...stress and stuff."

Sam nodded. "That's good. Does it?"

Wyatt didn't respond to that. He wanted to. He wanted to tell Sam that he'd started running to try to put distance between the two of them. To try to take some of the ache out of his chest by transferring it to his legs and his lungs through grueling miles. That it had helped him get physically stronger, but that he still felt like he could crumble at the mere presence of Sam in his space. Instead, he tried to redirect the conversation back to its original

33

track. He needed to get dressed. And he really needed Sam to leave his room. If he didn't, Wyatt was in danger of falling completely apart on day one of a week he swore he'd hold it together throughout. "What did you want to talk about?"

"Oh," Sam said. "I just don't want it to be weird between us this week."

Wyatt's chest clenched. He didn't want that either, but how could it not be? He'd told Sam he loved him, and Sam had told him that he was in love with someone else. Then, he'd broken up with that someone else, and they still weren't together. If that wasn't rejection, Wyatt didn't know what was. And what made it worse was that before the whole "confessing feelings" debacle, they'd been best friends. The tell-each-other-everything, spend-lazy-Sundays-doing-laundry-and-running errands-together kind of best friends. So, Wyatt had not only put his heart out there for Sam to completely shatter, but he'd also lost his best friend. Sam hadn't even told Wyatt when he'd broken up with Blair. Wyatt had had to hear about it from his uncle, which was not only humiliating, but hurtful. He'd clearly gone from being Sam's closest confidant to being nothing to him at all. Not even someone worthy of sharing major life updates with.

And now Sam wanted to talk about not making things weird. Seriously? There was no avoiding the weirdness. The only thing they could do, as far as Wyatt was concerned, was to pretend it wasn't weird. Grin and bear the awkwardness for the sake of everyone around them. That had been Wyatt's plan all along. But here was Sam trying to confront things. And that cut even deeper. The fact that Sam wasn't hurting like Wyatt was, that he didn't ache at the sight of him—hell, the fact that Sam seemed completely unaffected, was proof that Sam had never felt the way Wyatt did, and he never would.

"It won't be weird," Wyatt said, picking up his stack of clothing. He faked a smile for Sam. "We're good, Sam. Really."

Sam held his gaze, and Wyatt felt millimeters away from sobbing. But he didn't. He held the cheerful mask in place despite feeling like he couldn't so much as breathe without breaking down.

Sam eventually nodded. "Okay," he said, still holding eye contact. "I'll let you get dressed then." He turned to go, but stopped in the doorway, and Wyatt bit back a groan at the effort to keep it together any longer. Sam turned to look over his shoulder. "I like your longer hair," he said quietly. "You look really handsome." Then he turned and left, softly pulling the door closed behind him.

Wyatt let out the breath he'd been holding, and the tears started falling before he was back in the bathroom. He locked the bathroom door and turned on the sink's tap. He let the water flow in an attempt to muffle the sounds of his sobs. He'd let himself have a few minutes to let it all out. Expel the hurt from his body. Accept that Sam wasn't hurting the way he was. Steel himself to face the rest of the week. He gripped the edge of the vanity, his shoulders bunched in tense knots, and let the sobs escape him in choppy, jagged waves.

When the tears slowed, he wiped his face and ran his hands through his still damp hair. He pulled the towel from his waist and hung it on the bar near the shower. He focused on his breathing, taking four seconds to inhale, holding his breath for seven seconds, then releasing it for eight. He put on his boxers, then sat on the toilet lid to pull his socks on. Four second inhale, hold for seven, eight second exhale. He stood and stepped into his pants—in, hold, out—then pulled his T-shirt on. He tied his hair back into a black elastic, still continuing his breathing pattern as he stared at his reflection in the mirror. His face was a little blotchy from the crying, but overall, he looked presentable. His heart had slowed back down to almost normal, and the tears had stopped.

Wyatt exited the bathroom and took his time unpacking the rest of the items in his suitcase. He'd already hung up his suit for the wedding and a few other shirts. He lined up his dress shoes, running shoes, and sneakers neatly in the closet below them. He emptied the rest of his clothing into the empty chest of drawers. He placed the book he'd brought on the bedside table along with his glasses case. He stowed his now-empty suitcase in the closet, as well. Putting his items in their proper places helped calm him just as much as the breathing exercise had. He was feeling quite a bit better. He stood at the window in his room, looking out at the mountains. He was spending a week in a beautiful, scenic place. He was going to be surrounded by friends and family. He was celebrating the marriage of two people who were very important to him. It wasn't all bad. Not by a long shot.

He wouldn't make it weird. He could be around Sam for a week. He had to be okay with it. There was no alternative. He'd let himself have his meltdown, and now he was over it. He was well on his way to being over Sam. He could do this. Sam wasn't affected by him? He wouldn't be affected by Sam, either.

# Chapter Five

## Sam

Dan walked into the sunlit kitchen with an incredibly impressive scowl. He carried a large paper bag in one hand, and when Sam looked up from his cereal, he grinned. "You got them?" He spun around on his stool to face Dan, his eager golden retriever expression bordering on giddy.

Dan flung the bag at him, and Sam scrambled to catch it. "I can't believe you made me do that."

"I offered to go myself," Sam said. "And you were all, 'I don't think that's a good idea, Sam. I'd need to check out the place first, Sam.' So, I was simply making your job easier by sending you." He smiled sweetly at Dan, then he pulled the shoebox from the bag, sliding his cereal out of the way and flipping the lid of the box open. "Oh." Sam frowned down at the pair of black running shoes.

"What?" Dan's voice threatened violence. "What's the problem?"

"Oh, nothing," Sam said quickly, removing the first of the shoes, pulling the paper out of it, and untying the laces.

Dan went around the island and opened the fridge, pulling out a carton of eighteen eggs. "It's just...," Sam started. Dan gave him the classic Dan Death Stare that had most grown adults cowering under its power. But not Sam Deerwood. He simply flashed his freckle-faced smile and continued. "I'd asked for white. But it's all good, Big Dan. Thanks for getting them."

Dan held the classic Dan Death Stare on Sam a few beats, but he ultimately chose not to acknowledge that last bit. Eventually, Sam went on unpackaging his shoes, and Dan proceeded to make a five-egg omelet for himself.

They had the kitchen to themselves for a while, considering the early hour. Sam hadn't been able to sleep much the night before. Seeing Wyatt again had rattled him. And when he'd attempted to talk to Wyatt, things had gone from weird to worse in no time. Wyatt had been completely unaffected by Sam, and it had absolutely gutted Sam to see it. Wyatt not only looked different with his long hair and his crazy-cut body, but he no longer held the softness in his eyes for Sam that Sam now understood he'd taken for granted. His smile had been tight, and he'd seemed to want nothing more than for Sam to leave him alone. It had hurt. But Sam knew that he deserved it. And it was going to be work to get back on Wyatt's good side. But he would. He had to. Thus, him having Dan call one of the sporting goods shops in downtown Vail the night before asking if they'd open their doors at 5:00 a.m. for Sam Deerwood to shop before their regular hours. While Sam didn't make a habit of dropping his name to get special treatment, he had no qualms about it if it was for a good cause. And getting some running shoes before Wyatt woke up and went on his morning run was certainly a worthy cause.

Sam had casually asked Bowen about the run he'd gone on with Wyatt the previous day. Sam had pretended to be interested in the sights he'd seen, but he'd also asked a few probing questions about their running plans for the rest of the week. *You know, just out of curiosity.* When Bowen had mentioned Wyatt wanting to run in the mornings, and that he probably wouldn't be joining him because he didn't wake up before 7:00, Sam had formed his plan.

Wilkinson, the other bodyguard in the house, was the next person to appear in the kitchen, and Dan had acknowledged him with a head nod, a "morning," and a gruff, "there's eggs." Sam was endlessly amused by watching his personal security agent interact with others of his kind. Wilkinson was six feet two and full of lean muscle. He had dark hair, dark eyes, and absolutely looked like Keanu Reeves. If Keanu was part wolverine. Even in the wee hours of the morning, Wilkinson's perma-scowl game was solid. While Dan was a big, muscly teddy bear, Wilkinson was scary in a super sexy way. That's why Sam dubbed him Mean Keanu. Not that he'd ever tell Wilkinson that. He didn't want to get his ass kicked.

Sam quietly worked on lacing the sneakers while Dan and Wilkinson shared security plans for the day over massive amounts of eggs. There were two other big-name celebrities set to arrive later that day, Grayson Winter and Finn Everett. They were Hollywood's gay "it" couple. And Jasper, one of the grooms, was at least partially to thank for both of their superstar careers. Jasper was also a surrogate big brother figure to them. That had made Sam like Jasper early on. Of course, he had been skeptical. No one was likely to be good enough for his big brother Matty. But when Sam had seen that Jasper was not only business savvy, a complete genius when it came to TV production, and a stone-cold, almost-silver fox, but also a kind mentor to young people in the business, Sam had come around. Even if Jasper hadn't been the man to give Sam his very own big break, he'd like the guy. And if anyone was close to good enough for Matty, it was Jasper.

Sam had been zoning out a bit, lost in his thoughts, when he heard Wilkinson say, "Seems like overkill, but I can come along if we're back no later than nine."

"Thanks," Dan said to Wilkinson.

"Wait." Sam narrowed his eyes at Dan. "You do not need to drag Wilkinson along. It's just a run. There will likely be no one else out there. Maybe an elderly person walking their dog. Don't make this unnecessarily complicated, Dan-o."

Dan didn't respond, but his jaw ticked.

"I could use the exercise," Wilkinson grumbled, picking up his now-empty plate and bringing it over to the dishwasher.

Sam groaned in Dan's direction. "You're going to act like an overprotective Papa Bear this whole trip, aren't you?" He hung his head as he asked the question.

He wasn't even a little surprised when Dan put his plate into the dishwasher beside Wilkinson's and grunted a "That's right," as he came back around the island and passed Sam. "I'll be ready in five," he said as he disappeared down the hall. Wilkinson followed after him.

Five minutes later, Sam, Dan, and Wilkinson were out on the front patio stretching. Sam hadn't exactly thought through the running part beyond getting the shoes. Now that he was feeling the pull on his hamstrings from just the barest stretch, he was starting to dread the actual jogging part. He didn't even know the last time he'd run more than a few yards for a scene on set. And then there were the Grouchy Brothers twisting around their bulging muscles like they were freaking pretzels. Sam had assumed that someone with Dan's bulk would not be flexible. But apparently, he was wrong. He took a second to admire the sight of Dan and Wilkinson in their body-hugging running gear. They were both extremely hot men. But neither of them did it for Sam quite the way Wyatt did.

And dirty-thoughts-of-the-devil, the front door opened just at that moment, and Wyatt emerged in running shoes, sweats, and a snug fleece zip up. He didn't immediately see the others on the patio to the right of the sidewalk, which gave Sam a second to just appreciate how beautiful he looked in the first rays of early morning sun. Wyatt hummed to himself as he lifted his arms to tie his hair back from his face, his eyes on the horizon. Yeah. Even Dan and Wilkinson didn't hold a candle to Wyatt. No one did. Not for Sam, anyway.

Sam was caught red handed when Wyatt turned his head, his eyes widening as he registered there were others outside. Wyatt's gaze locked with Sam's, and Sam would have given anything to be able to decipher his expression.

"Oh," Wyatt said, confusion in his tone. "What are you guys doing?" It wasn't accusatory. Simple curiosity, it seemed.

"We were about to go for a run," Sam said, as casually as he could manage. "You know, check out the trails, get a peek at downtown." He trailed off as Wyatt's expression turned slightly suspicious.

"You run?" He raised one dark eyebrow. That was definitely suspicious.

"I run," Sam said, not able to fully disguise his defensiveness. It didn't help that Dan snorted behind him.

Wyatt nodded slowly. "Okay," he said.

"So, I'll just run with you, if you're going," Sam said. "You can show me the trail."

"You guys want to run with me?" Wyatt was addressing Dan and Wilkinson, and Sam swore to the muscle-bound gods that if Dan or Wilkinson foiled his plan, he'd hide their protein powder.

Neither Dan nor Wilkinson said anything, but both of them looked to Sam. Sam grinned at Wyatt. "We do."

Sam struggled to keep pace with Wyatt, despite the fact he knew Wyatt was going half speed on his behalf. But Sam was a professional actor. He could pull off oh-no-my-lungs-aren't-burning-at-all better than most. They'd run down a winding path that zigzagged downhill, leading them through the aspen-lined trail toward downtown Vail. Dan and Wilkinson chatted quietly a few yards behind Wyatt and Sam. Sam felt more than a little smug that they'd only passed two other hikers, both of whom were at least sixty years old and using trekking poles. Sam wasn't under any illusions that the older hikers couldn't outpace him on their worst day, but they didn't serve as a security threat, and that was what mattered. He'd argued with Dan that having two bodyguards accompany him on this early morning jog was overkill. And he'd been right. And Sam liked few things more than proving Dan wrong. The big guy was so fun to rattle. It was true that when Sam had first hired Dan, he'd appreciated Dan's thoroughness. His overkill had put Sam at ease when he'd first started getting overwhelmed by fans while out in public. But since he'd gone months without any real scares with fans or anyone else, sometimes he thought Dan could stand to pull the stick a tiny bit out of his ass. Not all the way, but maybe an inch or two.

When they reached downtown, Sam was thankful for the few stoplights that slowed them up long enough for him to catch his breath. The cobblestone streets and the businesses lining them were so charming they didn't seem real. Sam had only seen a town this well-kept and picturesque on the lot where he filmed *Ominous*. Their show took place on a set that Sam thought they'd used to film *Gilmore Girls* back in the day. There were a few slight changes, but the premise of *Ominous* was that a picture-perfect town had a dark secret. So, it had to look like a delightful, quiet place where everyone would want to live, only to later discover that there were all sorts of paranormal secrets behind the facade.

"You're quiet this morning." Wyatt had broken the silence Sam had been using to catch his breath.

"Oh," Sam said. "Yeah. I was just taking it all in."

"It's beautiful here, isn't it?" Wyatt didn't look at Sam when he spoke; he simply jogged along the trail that took them past shops that weren't yet open for the day.

"It is," Sam agreed. "Kind of reminds me of the *Ominous* set. You know, but real."

"I bet Jasper was pulling from Vail when he created the town," Wyatt said.

"I hadn't thought of that," Sam said, doing his best to keep his words from sounding too breathless.

Wyatt peeked at Sam from the corner of his eye and pointed toward an area with benches and large floral planters. "Want to sit a minute?"

"Yes," Sam agreed quickly. "Please."

Wyatt smiled and led the way to the seating area, plopping down on one of the benches.

"Don't you need to cool down or something?" Sam joined him, sitting beside him on the bench. "Isn't it bad to just stop running?"

Wyatt raised a brow and watched as Sam's chest heaved in the deliciously crisp air. "I thought you ran?"

"I do," Sam said. "Occasionally. That's how I know about cooldowns."

"I see," Wyatt said, his lips quirked up in a half-smirk-half-smile. "Well, that jog through town was my cooldown."

Sam glared at him but couldn't hold the expression long before his own grin burst through. "Jackass," he said, swatting Wyatt with the back of his hand.

Dan and Wilkinson had caught up to them, but they didn't sit. They stood a bit back from them, giving them some much appreciated space.

"How is work going?" Wyatt asked.

"It's good," Sam said. "I love it a little more every day. I still can't believe I get to be an actor for a living. It's unreal."

"You're talented," Wyatt said. "I'm not surprised in the least."

The sincerity in his voice had Sam a bit choked up. Wyatt had always believed in him. More than he'd believed in himself most times. And sitting here with him, joking and just talking—Sam had missed this. Despite the complicated feelings he had for Wyatt and the strain on their relationship over the last year, the bottom line was that this was what he missed most. Being with his best friend.

Sam managed to speak after a few seconds. "Thanks," he said. He wasn't sure he could manage more than that. If he started talking, too many feelings threatened to sabotage this tentative moment.

Sam looked at Wyatt, who was already looking at him. Sam could see warring emotions battling it out in Wyatt's inscrutable hazel eyes. He wondered if they were the same feelings trying to claw their way to the surface from Sam's own heart. But that was too much to even hope. Sam didn't let himself go there. He'd learned that lesson. He was always like this—he romanticized things too much. He felt too intensely. He jumped too hastily. He loved too recklessly. And he had the scars to prove it.

# Chapter Six

## Wyatt

For a moment there, Wyatt had almost forgotten that any time had passed since the last time he and Sam had just hung out like best friends. Initially, Wyatt had been annoyed that Sam and his bodyguards had ambushed him to tag along on his run. It was strange that Sam couldn't even go for an early-morning jog on a mostly deserted trail without needing two enormous and lethal chaperones. But after a while, he and Sam had fallen into step both literally and figuratively, and they'd chatted and laughed like nothing had changed. But then they'd been alerted by one of Sam's escorts that they needed to turn back, and Wyatt was jolted back to reality. Things weren't the same. Sam was famous now. And he and Wyatt had not been best friends for some time, no matter how much he wished they still could be.

As they approached the rental house, two new SUVs were parked in front of the garage. One of the bodyguards, Wilkinson, was tapping away on his phone. "Hicks is here. Says we need to rearrange some things," Wilkinson said, presumably to Dan, but Sam and Wyatt could hear him as well.

"Why?" Dan asked. "We don't need to rearrange anything."

"He says there are more Deerwoods on the premises than initially anticipated. They took the room we were going to put Winter and Everett in."

Dan sighed. "Wonderful," he said, his deep voice somehow both monotone and dripping in sarcasm.

"What do you mean more Deerwoods?" Sam had wedged his way between Dan and Wilkinson as they made their way up the driveway.

Wilkinson didn't immediately respond.

Sam pressed. "The only Deerwood left to arrive is my sister," Sam said. "And her plus one."

Wilkinson coughed and faced forward, avoiding Sam's eyes.

"Fine," Sam said, charging in front of them to reach the door first. "I'll find out for myself."

Once inside, they could hear the newcomers before they could see them. There was the sound of loud laughter, excited voices, and—was that a...a baby crying in the background?

"Mara!" Sam called out his sister's name as he barreled into the dining room to wrap his arms around his sister.

"Gross, Sam! You're all sweaty!" Mara pushed Sam away from her, but she had an affectionate smile for him.

Wyatt had toed off his running shoes by the door and slowly followed Sam and the bodyguards into the dining room where the newcomers were apparently gathered. When he entered the room, Mara squealed and scurried toward him.

"Wyatt!" She squeezed him into a hug.

"Hey!" Sam protested. "You literally just shoved me away for being sweaty, but Wyatt gets a bear hug?"

Mara held onto Wyatt for a second longer before stepping back and addressing her brother. "I've missed him!"

Sam looked supremely offended. "What about me?"

Mara shrugged a shoulder as a tall, dark, and handsome man entered the dining area and raised a hand in greeting. "Hey, everyone," he said.

"What's up, Tyson," Sam said, nodding to his sister's boyfriend.

Then Tyson approached Wyatt, and they did their custom handshake, which ended in their usual fist bump. "How was the flight?"

"Not great," Tyson said with a cringe.

"Why not?" Wyatt pulled out a chair and sat, joining various members of the rental house's inhabitants who were sipping coffee around the massive table.

"That'd be my fault," a woman's voice said from the doorway. In walked Harlow Benson, an actress friend of the Deerwood family's from back in LA. Wyatt tried not to register his surprise at seeing her in Vail. She wasn't particularly close to either of the grooms, so her presence seemed a bit odd, even though Wyatt knew her to be...er...close with Mara and Tyson, a fact Sam was yet unaware of, Wyatt was pretty sure. "Or rather Milo's," Harlow explained. "Toddlers don't necessarily like sitting still in a confined space for long stretches of time."

"Did you get him down?" Mara asked as she pulled out a chair that Harlow sat in.

Harlow sighed. "I think so," she said. Milo's cries had died down, so it was possible the kid was settling down. Tyson walked up behind Harlow and rested his large hands on her narrow shoulders, gently squeezing them. Sam's eyes darted from his sister's boyfriend's fingers massaging another woman right in front of her to his sister's shockingly content expression as she looked on. In fact, Mara took the seat beside Harlow and placed a hand on her knee.

"He'll sleep," Mara assured Harlow, who smiled up at Mara with warmth.

Sam's eyes leapt from Tyson's hands on Harlow's shoulders to his soft smile for Mara, who smiled up at him before giving Harlow's knee a pat. Sam turned wide saucer eyes to Wyatt that practically screamed "Are you seeing this?" Wyatt looked at the table. Nuh uh. He wasn't touching this.

"Excuse me," Sam said, turning back toward Mara and company. "But what the hell is going on here?"

Wyatt felt his cheeks flush. He didn't want to get in the middle of this. He kept his eyes on the wooden tabletop, pretending to be especially interested in the grain of the wood.

Mara looked up at Sam and rolled her eyes. "Sam."

"What?"

"Don't act all clueless."

Sam spun to look at Wyatt again, who still avoided making eye contact.

"I am clueless," Sam said to Mara. "I have no idea why your boyfriend's hands are on your friend, and you seem unbothered by it. Or why you're squeezing her thigh like that's normal," he added, nodding to Harlow's lap. "Or—and I mean no offense, Harlow, I'm always happy to see you and Milo—why Harlow's even here."

Mara looked up at the ceiling like she was asking for patience from above. After a few seconds of her not responding, she looked at her bewildered younger brother. "We're together, Sam. You knew that."

"You and Tyson, yes. I did know that. That's why I'm

49

concerned that he's feeling up Harlow right now." Sam glared at Tyson, who lifted his hands off Harlow's shoulders in a "don't shoot" gesture.

"And Harlow," Mara said. She sounded more than a little exasperated. "Why do you think she always spends the night at my place? Why we have a room for Milo there? Jesus, Sam. You've known we were together for ages."

Sam once again looked from his sister to Harlow, to Tyson, back to Mara.

"Surely you knew," Mara said. "Everyone did."

Sam looked at Wyatt again, who shrugged helplessly.

"So, you're like a throuple or something?"

"Exactly like a throuple," Mara said, reaching out to grab Harlow's hand and squeeze it. Tyson put his hands back on Harlow's shoulders. All three of them looked at Sam, smiling.

"But then—" Sam looked around like he expected someone to jump out and yell that he'd been on candid camera. "Why didn't Dan expect them then?" he asked, nodding toward Harlow.

"Because we didn't think we could make it," Harlow explained. "I wasn't sure I could get the time off."

"But—"

"Sam." Wyatt had gotten up and stood next to Sam. It was clear that Sam was a bit blindsided, whether he should have been or not, and Wyatt had gone into soothing mode without even realizing it. He looked at Sam, speaking softly. "It's nice, isn't it? That they're all so happy?"

Sam looked at Wyatt, who smiled patiently at Sam, hoping to ease some of the tension and calm Sam's racing mind. Sam nodded, like he knew Wyatt was right. And if Sam thought about it, Wyatt knew he'd put the pieces in place. Mara and Harlow did spend an awful lot of time together. And Harlow and Tyson had a ton of chemistry when they'd been in a play together. And Tyson and Mara definitely had a good thing going. It all kind of...made sense. Wyatt might not be great at relationships, but he was a believer in evidence he could see. And the three of them seemed to be a happy unit.

Sam nodded again and addressed his sister. "It is. Nice. That you all have each other. Sorry if I reacted weirdly just now." Wyatt reached out and squeezed Sam's shoulder.

"It's okay," Mara said. "Your cluelessness is endearing. Sometimes," she added. Mara shared a look with Wyatt, as if to say, "Don't we all know how infuriating Sam's clueless-ness can be too?" but he didn't have time to dwell on that because the kitchen was filling with more people—Sam's brothers, their partners, a handful of bodyguards. It was going to be a full house.

Everyone greeted the Mara throuple, and they started discussing the wedding plans and the new sleeping arrange-ments since Harlow and Milo had been able to make it after all. Two gorgeous men that Wyatt had seen a few times back in LA, but more often on billboards or on the big screen, wandered in from somewhere in the house. Grayson Winter and Finn Everett. Wyatt did his level best to not act starstruck. But they were two of the most famous men in Hollywood, America's favorite gay "it" couple, and they were basically every gay boy's fantasy wrapped up in freak-ishly fit bodies with dazzling white smiles. Sometimes Wyatt took for granted that his uncle had married into a family that rubbed elbows with superstars like Grayson and Finn. And now they were just hanging out in a rental lodge with Wyatt and his family like it was totally normal. And, aside from the bodyguards, it kind of was. Grayson and

Finn were two of the most down-to-earth, cool guys Wyatt had met in LA.

Everyone mingled in the kitchen/dining area for a while, opening cans of sparkling water and laughing, discussing the scenery and the drive up from the airport. In the hubbub, Wyatt had lost Sam, who had drifted over to where his sister and brothers were chatting.

After a few minutes, Hicks, the bodyguard that had arrived while Wyatt had been on the run, hollered out, "Listen up, everyone." He was standing in front of the massive stone fireplace that was the focal point of the enormous great room. Everyone filed into the room, sitting on the sofa or standing behind it, perching in armchairs, and turned their attention to Hicks, the oldest and most intimidating of the bodyguard trio in the house. He held up his phone. "I have the new rooming assignments here. They are nonnegotiable. If you have a problem with it, no you don't."

Wyatt's eyes widened and he looked to Matt, who stood with his arms wrapped around Jasper's middle, looking all moony at his husband-to-be. Apparently, Matt and Jasper didn't give a shit where anyone else slept as long as they had their grooms' suite to themselves. After a few more minutes of Hicks giving some general instructions, which basically amounted to, "Don't post on social media and don't talk to anyone in town" about who was staying at the lodge unless they wanted to answer to Hicks, the meeting was adjourned.

Wyatt slipped away to take a shower. He was feeling a little overwhelmed by all the new arrivals, and his blood pressure had spiked when it finally dawned on Sam that his sister was in a polyamorous relationship that Wyatt had clearly known about and never pointed out to Sam. But Wyatt knew that wasn't on him. It's not like they'd actually been talking recently. Maybe if they had been, Sam would be more up to speed on what was happening. It wasn't lost on Wyatt that he'd been more in the know about the goings-on of Sam's family than Sam was. But when things had... gone down with Sam and Wyatt, Sam's siblings had never let that affect their relationships with him. And Wyatt had truly appreciated that. The Deerwoods were his family now, too, whether he and Sam were speaking or not.

Once in the quiet of his room, Wyatt let out a deep breath, releasing the tension he hadn't consciously realized he'd been holding in his shoulders. Wyatt felt thankful that he wasn't a celebrity. He didn't have to deal with body-guards telling him what to do and watching his every move. It was all just too much. Sure, he hadn't particularly minded having them tag along on his run earlier, but that was probably because he only dealt with it for a few hours. He could leave and find some solitude, unlike Grayson, Finn, and Sam, who would always have a burly, stone-faced man shadowing their every move. Yes, Wyatt enjoyed being just an average, unfamous guy who could simply slip away to his own room, get into his own shower, and get away from all the chaos. He had the fleeting thought that there'd been a time he'd willingly have given up any semblance of privacy and peace if it meant being with Sam, but since that was not an option anyway, he chose to look on the bright side; he was a nobody, and he was thankful for that.

# Chapter Seven

## Sam

Sam noticed Dan, Wilkinson, and Hicks huddled together, and he wandered over, taking the spot to Dan's left. If there was a HO Security meeting happening, Sam wanted in.

He'd just listened to Hicks give the rundown of all the security measures that would be taken for the rest of the week, including threats of bodily harm to anyone who leaked a word of anything about his A-list clients' whereabouts. Sam was ready to check in with Dan about whether any of this had anything to do with him, or if he could simply go about his business.

"What's the plan, Dan?"

Hicks and Wilkinson excused themselves with a last nod to Dan, and Dan turned to address Sam. "You're moving," he said.

"Oh yeah? Did I get demoted now that I'm not the most famous person in the lodge?"

"Basically," Dan said, straight faced.

Sam gave him an affronted look, and Dan started

walking toward the hallway. "Follow me," he said. "We'll move your stuff."

Sam scampered after him. "Where am I moving?"

"You're sharing a room now," Dan said.

"Ooh, with you, Big Dan? Do I get to see if you wear pajamas with little mugs of beer on them? Or is it the actual *Cheers* logo? Would that be too on the nose?"

Dan went into the room Sam had been using, and Sam followed. Sam could see that different luggage had been wheeled in already, like they were just waiting for him to vacate.

"If you can pack up, I'll bring your stuff down to the new room," Dan said.

"Okay, okay," Sam said. "I'll make room for the real movie stars." Sam quickly packed the few things he'd taken out, not really caring about being moved. He was amenable.

Ten minutes later, Dan wheeled the bigger of the two suitcases, and Sam followed him down the hallway. "So, who am I sharing with?" Sam finally asked. "Don't say Mara's throuple and their baby, Dan. Do not say that."

Dan chuckled and turned the corner. "No," he said, and Sam felt the nerves start to jitter in his belly. They were heading down the hall that led to Wyatt's room. Sure enough, Dan stopped in front of Wyatt's door and knocked.

A few seconds later, the door swung open and there was Wyatt. Sam couldn't help the grin that broke across his face at the sight of Wyatt's shower-damp hair and slightly confused expression.

"Yes?" He addressed Dan, but his eyes flicked to Sam. And the suitcases.

"You have a new roommate," Dan said.

Wyatt's eyes widened as he looked from Dan to Sam to

the suitcase before returning to Sam and lingering there. "Oh," Wyatt said. "Um. Are you sure?"

Sam wasn't sure if Wyatt was asking Dan whether he was sure he had the right rooming arrangements, or if he was asking Sam if he was sure he wanted to room with him. In any case, Sam answered before Dan could.

"'Fraid so," he said, flashing Wyatt the boyish grin he knew full well was exceedingly charming.

Wyatt took a beat before responding, and Sam thought he heard him mutter something under his breath, but before he knew it, Wyatt was stepping back and pulling the door open wide. "Then by all means," he said, gesturing them into the room.

Sam was pretty sure Dan shook his head at Wyatt or him, or the both of them, though it wasn't clear if it was in frustration, amusement, or a combination of the two. Dan wheeled Sam's bag into the room, parking it in front of the closet. Sam wandered in holding his other bag awkwardly, not certain where to put it. Dan walked over to Sam and clapped him on the shoulder. "Well, I'm just down the hall. Do not, under any circumstances, leave this house without me. And stay off social media."

Sam rolled his eyes. "I know the drill, Daniel Day Lewis."

Dan eyed him a second longer, then turned to address Wyatt. "And if this joker gives you any trouble, you let me know."

Wyatt saluted Dan. "Aye, aye." Wyatt had a broad smile for Dan. "You know I will."

With that, Dan left, closing the door behind him.

Then Wyatt and Sam were alone in the room. Sam looked around the space, searching for something to say or do to make the situation less awkward. Wyatt hadn't asked for Sam to room with him, of that Sam was sure. But Wyatt did seem to be taking it in stride. But that was probably less to do with Sam and more to do with Wyatt's nature. He never wanted to cause waves or rock the boat. He was the ultimate team player.

Sam reached the large French doors that opened to a small balcony that overlooked the mountains. He peered through the glass out at the expanse of blue sky and white-capped peaks. "Sorry about this," Sam said, not looking at Wyatt.

"It's not your fault," Wyatt said. "Hicks leaves no room for discussion when he makes his plans."

"It's a HO's world, and we're all just living in it."

Wyatt chuckled, and the sound made Sam feel lighter inside. Sam set his bag down on the floor in front of the doors and turned to Wyatt. "You know Hicks then? I've only seen him a couple of times."

Wyatt nodded. "Yeah. Grayson and Finn sometimes come to the cafe after hours with some of their cast and crew. Hicks and/or Wilkinson is usually in tow."

Sam nodded. "Makes sense."

"You hit the security jackpot with Danson," Wyatt said as he sat on the edge of the bed. "He's the coolest one, for sure."

Sam chuckled. "I don't think 'cool' is the word I'd use to describe the big guy, but I definitely like him. We get along." Sam hovered around the room's periphery, not sure where to sit or stand or what to do with his hands. There was a narrow fireplace to the right of the French doors, a small gas fire flickering inside. To the left of the doors was an armchair, and Sam briefly contemplated sitting there. Then a thought struck him that had him surveying the rest of the room with new curiosity. With the French doors to his back, he saw the door that led to the hallway on his right. To his left, the entrance to the en suite. Directly in front of him, adorned with a minimalistic headboard, was one king-sized bed. Wyatt was still perched on the edge of it, his eyes on his own knees, like he was avoiding looking at Sam.

"Is there…" Sam wasn't sure how to ask his question. On the one hand, he really wanted the information, but on the other, he didn't want to give Wyatt the impression he didn't want to be close to him. Because he did. He really, really did.

"What?" Wyatt's eyes met Sam's, and Sam's heart thumped faster.

"Is there a cot or something? Or do we…"

Wyatt's cheeks flamed red. "It's a king, so we could probably just…"

"Share?" Sam asked, praying that his voice didn't sound too pathetically hopeful.

"I mean, there's plenty of room." Wyatt shrugged. "And I don't want to bother Jasper and Matt by asking for a cot. They have more than enough going on."

Sam fought hard not to break out into a massive grin. Luckily, he was a professional actor. Instead, he nodded. "True. The way Matty was freaking out over those bouton-nieres was bad enough."

Wyatt laughed. "They turned out surprisingly decent-ly," he said.

Sam puffed up his chest. "No big deal, but I know my way around some floral tape."

For a long minute, Sam let himself stare at Wyatt's smiling face. He felt his own grin stretch his cheeks, and he let it happen. Wyatt's hazel eyes crinkled at the corners, and his long hair hung over his forehead to one side before Wyatt absently pushed it out of his face. Looking past the changes in Wyatt's appearance—the hair and the sharper lines of his cheekbones and jaw—Sam could see the same Wyatt he'd initially fallen for. It was the sometimes-too-serious boy who carried pain and loss in those beautiful eyes. The one whose genuine smile was a rare gift that a precious few people ever got to see. Sam had always known he was lucky to witness it. He supposed he just never expressed his gratitude to Wyatt, and he should have. Maybe he could now. If it wasn't too late. Before he could think of what to say, Wyatt looked away, pointing toward the en suite.

"I'm done in there if you want to shower or anything," he said. "I think I'm going to check my email quickly and then find something to eat." He stood from the bed and lifted his laptop from the top of a dresser, bringing it back to the bed and placing it on his lap. He opened it and began plucking away at the keys without another look at Sam. *Well, I'm dismissed,* Sam thought, picking up his bag and taking it into the bathroom.

Sam took his time in the shower and working through his skincare routine. He wasn't particularly vain, but he knew how good high-def TVs were these days. You could see every pore on his face on some of them. After finishing up with his moisturizer, he set it on the right side of the vanity with his other toiletries. Wyatt had laid claim to the left side of the vanity, and Sam couldn't help but inspect the neat row of items Wyatt had set out. Sam knew he hadn't expected to be sharing a room, but he still kept things neat and tidy, as was his way. Sam smiled as he recognized the toothpaste and deodorant brands Wyatt had always used. He liked seeing that some things about Wyatt hadn't changed. His eye caught on a small, dark blue glass bottle. Sam walked over and picked it up. *Huh.* He lifted the cologne to his nose and sniffed it. *That was strange.* He'd never known Wyatt to wear cologne. He'd said something once about it making him feel nauseated and giving him a headache. Sam set the bottle back down carefully where he'd found it, not sure what to make of the fact that it was the exact same cologne he had in his own toiletry kit. Weird coincidence.

* * *

That evening, after long hours of talking and laughing and eating delicious food they'd had delivered from a local restaurant, Sam wandered down the hall toward his new room around one in the morning. Sam wasn't sure what time Wyatt had snuck away, but he'd been certain the amount of people-ing throughout the day had to have worn him right out. And, if Sam was honest, part of the reason he'd stayed up so late was to avoid going back to their shared room. It wasn't that he didn't want to be there—it was more that he really, really did. He wanted to be alone with Wyatt, sharing a bed with him. The thing was, he just really wished it were under different circumstances. Like ones where Wyatt wasn't just allowing Sam to bunk with him because he was too kind to make a fuss about it. Sam had always imagined the first time he and Wyatt shared a bed properly, it would be because they'd finally sorted out their shit and found their way back to each other where they belonged. Not because of a celebrity-ridden lodging situation. Sam didn't know what to do with his mixed emotions of excitement and sadness, anticipation and regret. He was about to be in a situation he'd dreamed of countless times, but it was definitely not on the terms he'd imagined.

When he returned to the room, Sam found it dark save

for the bedside lamp on his side of the bed emitting soft, yellow light. Wyatt's lamp was already off, and he was tucked in, facing away from Sam. He didn't move or acknowledge Sam's presence, so Sam simply slipped into bed quietly and clicked off his own lamp.

In the silent darkness of the room, Sam's mind whirred. He wasn't sure he'd ever felt more confusing emotions in his life. On the one hand, he was happier than he'd been in months at the opportunity to be here with Wyatt. God, he'd missed him. But on the other, Wyatt was right there beside him—literally an arm's length away—but they were so far apart from where they'd once been. Sam could feel the distance between them like a cold, bottomless chasm. The thought of bridging that distance was all-consuming, but he was scared. Terrified even. At least where they stood now, they could see each other from the opposite banks. They might have space between them, but Wyatt was in his life. If he tried to bridge the gap, he might lose everything, free-falling into the abyss, and never see Wyatt's face again. He didn't think he could risk that. But at the same time, the urge to reach out and touch Wyatt felt like a physical ache in his body. It was like he knew. He just knew with everything in him that Wyatt was his soulmate. And he'd somehow managed to push him away. To turn them into this—not a couple, no longer best friends. Barely acquaintances whose uncle and brother were married to one another. Sam cursed himself for fucking things up like this. To the point that now Wyatt had a man bun and ran races and had cologne on his vanity and Sam had no part in it. It hurt.

Especially because he knew it was all his fault.

# Chapter Eight

## Wyatt

"This can't be right," Bowen said, stepping out into the hallway with a pair of dove gray dress pants plastered to his thighs and ass, the fly gaping open. "These could never contain all of this," he said, gesturing to the bulge that was clearly not fitting into the too-small pants.

"Gross," Wyatt said, walking out of his room into the hallway holding up a pair of far-too-large dress pants with both hands.

"Swapsies," Bowen said, bending down and tugging at the ankles of the pants, wiggling his way out of them right there in the hallway.

Wyatt looked both ways, really hoping to change anywhere but in the open, but thinking better of it. If he scurried back into his room to change, his uncle would certainly give him shit about it, and he just wasn't in the mood. Grumbling about how Bowen could have looked at the "W. Price" versus the "B. Price" on the garment bags before distributing the tuxes, Wyatt lowered the pants until he could step out of them. He stood awkwardly in the hallway, holding the pants in front of his body, which was now only covered in a pair of white boxer briefs and an undershirt. And Bowen was taking his sweet time, struggling out of the pants like he was wrestling a crocodile. Luckily, everyone else in the house seemed to be occupied with various wedding tasks or sightseeing. Most of them had tried on their tuxes earlier when Wyatt had been on his run. Bowen thudded into the wall as he worked the second pant leg over his heel. Wyatt was pretty sure that was sweat on his uncle's brow. Finally, he tugged the pants from his body, raising them in the air triumphantly. "There," he gasped. Wyatt shook his head and took the pants from Bowen, shoving the pair he'd been holding at his uncle.

"Well, well, well. What do we have here?"

Wyatt was certain he had a deer-in-the-headlights look on his face as he whipped his head toward the speaker. He was, unfortunately, bent over with his actual pants pulled up as far as his thighs when Clark and Sam walked into the hallway. Wyatt felt his cheeks flame, but he quickly pulled up the pants and fastened them. Bowen had done the same, both of them in properly fitted garments at last.

"I tried to squeeze my big ass into Wyatt's pants," Bowen explained to his husband with a shrug. "It wasn't happening."

Clark stepped up to Bowen and grabbed his shoulders, spinning him around so that his back was to Clark. Clark carefully inspected the fit of Bowen's pants as they snugly curved around his round ass cheeks. He slid his hands over Bowen's ass, his expression serious. Assessing. "These seem to be just about right," he said finally, whirling Bowen around and greeting him with a proper smile and kiss at last.

During this little display, Sam and Wyatt had stood there, fidgeting and averting their eyes from their relatives'

PDA. They glanced at one another out of the corner of their eyes, sharing a knowing look. This wasn't the first time they'd witnessed Clark and Bowen getting handsy in front of them. And it certainly wouldn't be the last. Wyatt rolled his eyes in mock exasperation, and Sam grinned.

"Yours look good, too," Sam said, nodding his head in Wyatt's direction.

"Oh," Wyatt said, looking down at the pants, noticing that they did seem to fit perfectly. "Thanks. They certainly fit better than Uncle Bo's big-ass pants." Wyatt smirked at Bowen, but Bowen was too wrapped up in Clark.

"You know you guys have a room right there," Sam said, pointing down the hall.

Bowen and Clark gave each other what could only be described as fuck-me eyes, and they were gone.

Sam and Wyatt both grinned. As much as he preferred not to witness it, Wyatt was truly happy that Clark and Bowen were so happy together. They deserved it.

"Do you need to try the rest of the suit?" Sam asked Wyatt.

Wyatt nodded, looking toward Bowen and Clark's closed door. "I do, but it's in their room, so…"

Sam laughed, and Wyatt felt warmth in his chest at the sound. He'd missed Sam's laugh so much in their time apart. The two of them started toward their shared room, and Wyatt swallowed hard, the nerves starting to prickle in his belly at the reminder of them sharing space. And a bed. The night before, Wyatt had slept all of maybe two hours, nonconsecutively. He'd been way too wired with Sam right there beside him. It had been dark, so he couldn't make out his features clearly, but he could feel his presence. His slow breathing, his Sam smell that Wyatt loved so much. The familiar beat of his heart that Wyatt could swear he could feel reflected in the rhythmic thump of his own. He knew he couldn't physically feel Sam's heart beating from across the bed, but ever since the day they'd met, Wyatt had felt that he knew Sam's heart somehow. That it spoke to his. And last night proved to him that the connection was still there, strong as it ever was.

Sam collapsed into the armchair in the corner of the room with a sigh. "I can't believe how much shit there is to do for a wedding," he commented to Wyatt, who was hovering near the bed where he'd left the pants hanger and the pants he'd been wearing before trying on the suit. Sam continued talking while Wyatt internally panicked about whether to take the hanger and the pants into the en suite, or if it would seem strange. Or would it be weirder to just change in front of Sam? They'd changed in front of one another often enough over the course of their friendship. But that had been before. "I've never even heard of most of the things Matty was saying were left to sort out. Apparently, he had a phone call about canapés he was stressing over. And he had me promise to help affix the swags to the arbor for the ceremony. Like what even language is he speaking? And then, when I naturally said, 'Oh, I've got swag,' he just scowled at me."

Wyatt decided to just change right there. Sam was speaking to him, after all. It would seem weirder to leave the room. Mind made up, he unbuttoned the suit pants. "I expect he's just nervous," Wyatt said to Sam over his shoulder. "Getting married is a big deal."

"Yeah," Sam said, his voice a bit further away. Wyatt peeked over his shoulder to see Sam staring out the window. He took the opportunity while Sam's eyes were averted to pull down and step out of the suit pants. "All I know," Sam went on, "is if I ever get married, we're doing the courthouse and..." Wyatt had picked up his own pants and was preparing to put them on when he realized Sam had stopped speaking. Wyatt froze. Without turning around, he knew Sam was looking at his pantsless body. A small thrill tingled through him. Sam was checking him out. He could feel his eyes on him. Sam coughed, and that slight tell of nervousness gave Wyatt inexplicable confidence. He knew he looked pretty good. Running had sculpted his thighs and toned his ass. He definitely wasn't the skinny guy he'd been the last time Sam had seen him undressed.

Wyatt slowly turned around to face Sam, knowing full well that his white boxer briefs were somewhat see-through. To his delight, he could actually see Sam swallow as his eyes took Wyatt in. Wyatt smirked. "You were saying?" He was aiming for casual with maybe a hint of teasing.

Sam's eyes rose from his lower body very, very slowly, and met his.

"I have no fucking clue what I was saying," Sam said, his lopsided grin confirming that he had, in fact, been checking Wyatt out, and that he was not in the least sorry about it.

Wyatt could feel his own smirk morphing into a wide smile. For some reason, the fact that Sam had been looking —and seemed to like what he saw—gave Wyatt a surge of pride. Somewhere in the back of his mind, he was annoyed that Sam's approval was what was feeding his confidence. He knew he should be confident and proud of himself regardless of Sam—and he was—but, damn, it felt good to have Sam's eyes trying their best to strip his boxers off from across the room.

"You look so good, Wyatt," Sam said. He nodded his head slowly, like he was agreeing with himself as he spoke. "So fucking hot." Wyatt felt his cock swell at the combination of Sam's words and the way his blue eyes seemed incapable of looking away. The arousal was helping him shed his inhibitions, and he tossed the pants he'd been holding back onto the bed. He placed his hands on his hips, effectively striking a pose.

"You think?" He looked down at his own body like he was assessing it.

"Oh, yeah," Sam said. "I think."

Their stares snagged on one another. Something was sparking between them as they searched each other's eyes. Wyatt could feel it, almost like a heavy bass line thrumming. His legs started to tremble slightly, and he attempted to root them more firmly to the floor. He was, after all, trying to pull off confidence. He had always known that Sam was attracted to him. Ever since Wyatt had first realized Sam was bisexual, the pieces started to fall into place—the way Sam's eyes lingered sometimes, the way his cheeks flushed when they'd sat close to one another. Even when he'd tried to act like he wasn't, Wyatt had known. The sexual tension had been palpable at times, even when they were just friends.

One night, about four months after they'd met, they'd been up late watching videos together on Sam's phone, lying side by side on their stomachs on Wyatt's bed. They'd both been laughing at what they were watching, and when the laughter died down, Sam was looking at him with the oddest expression. There was so much affection there, but there was also curiosity. And hunger. Wyatt remembered that Sam had looked at his lips, like he was struggling not to lean over and kiss them.

Or there'd been the night that the very first episode of *Ominous* aired, and all their family and friends had gathered to watch Sam on TV for the very first time. When the credits rolled at the end of the episode, everyone was cheering and congratulating Sam, and Sam had turned to Wyatt. Wyatt had pulled Sam into a squeezing hug, and Sam had held on several long seconds beyond what was normal for a friendly hug. He'd wrapped his arms around him like he wanted to keep him close forever. Wyatt would remember that hug for the rest of his life.

They'd never acted on the attraction. Not really. Wyatt had, of course, lost his mind and confessed to Sam that he was in love with him a few months after that hug. And Sam had told him he loved someone else, crushing Wyatt and his stupid heart into dust.

But Wyatt was not going to think about that. That was the past. And what he knew right now was that the attraction he'd seen glimmers of from Sam over the years was still there, blazing bright, unmistakable. And based on the way Sam's chest was rising and falling, and how his breath grew ragged as he stared at Wyatt's now fully hard cock stretching his white boxers, it might have even gotten stronger. Wyatt briefly had the thought that this was a terrible idea. Getting close to Sam, testing those waters, had only ever left him pulverized by unrequited feelings. But for the life of him, he couldn't make himself think logically. Instead, he took a deep breath, then stepped closer to Sam.

Sam widened his knees and rubbed his hands down his thighs, his eyes never once straying from Wyatt as he advanced toward him. Sam bit his bottom lip as Wyatt stepped within arm's reach of Sam.

"Wyatt," Sam said, his voice soft. His gaze traveled slowly up Wyatt's body until he was staring into Wyatt's eyes. "I..."

"What?" Wyatt asked, his voice sounding breathy. His legs were visibly trembling, as were his hands at his sides.

"I've always thought you were beautiful," Sam said, his face serious.

Wyatt felt his eyes sting, and he had to lighten the mood before he burst into embarrassing tears. "Even before I had muscles?" he asked playfully, turning to the side and flexing his calf for Sam.

"Yes," Sam said. "You are gorgeous no matter what."

Wyatt inched a bit closer, so his legs were nearly between Sam's widespread knees. He was aware that he was essentially presenting his junk right at Sam's eye level, but his body was moving on instinct, or maybe it was just surrendering to the magnetic pull he'd always felt toward Sam. Maybe just this once, he could stop fighting it. Wyatt felt like he was watching himself from above, his head swirling with desire and excitement and nerves. He reached out both of his arms, turning them palm up. Sam held his stare as he reached out and put his hands in Wyatt's. Wyatt sighed at the warm weight resting in his palms. He slid his palms over Sam's hands, his fingers reaching out to brush the delicate skin of Sam's wrists. "In that case," Wyatt said, trying his best to keep his voice steady enough to resume their conversation. He wasn't able to, so he simply pulled Sam's hands out at the same time he took another small step forward, placing Sam's palms on his bare thighs. Sam's soft hands immediately gripped him possessively, squeezing before sliding slowly up toward the legs of his boxers. Wyatt's dick leapt at the sight of Sam's face inches away and the feel of his fingers digging into the meat of his thighs before deliberately inching higher.

If Wyatt thought he'd been trembling before, it was nothing compared to this. He squeezed his eyes closed and tried to breathe. "Wyatt." Sam said his name like that was a long-lost answer to a question he'd had for ages. Sam's fingers had traveled to the back of Wyatt's thighs and were sliding up under the back of his boxers, grazing the bottom of each of his muscular ass cheeks. Sam groaned and pulled Wyatt in, resting his forehead on Wyatt's abs. A moan escaped Wyatt. He could feel Sam's soft hair on his stomach, hot breath warming his skin. He was dying for Sam to just pull his boxers down and grab his ass properly, but he didn't dare interrupt Sam's exploration. Sam spoke again, his voice muffled. "I need..."

Thud, thud, thud. "Sam!"

The knocks on the door had Sam dropping his hands and Wyatt leaping away from him.

"Sam!" Thud, thud. "Get your ass out here. You need to show us how to get the karaoke app to work on the TV."

As Mara was yelling through the door, Wyatt quickly pulled his pants on and ran his hands through his hair. Sam had reached the door, pulling it open. Wyatt couldn't see Mara from where he stood, but he heard Sam say, "I'll be right there. Give me two minutes." He shut the door and turned toward Wyatt.

"Sorry," Sam began. "Can..."

"It's okay," Wyatt said. "All good." He gave Sam his best "I'm not at all shook right now" smile. "Karaoke waits for no man."

# Chapter Nine

## Sam

Sam wiped his sweat-slick hair off his forehead as the room erupted in applause and whoops. As he always did, he'd left it all out there on the "stage" when he'd performed a high-energy rendition of "Alone" by Heart. The massive great room was actually crowded with the number of people gathered around the huge TV where the lyrics for the song had scrolled across the screen as he'd sung. Between the sheer number of bodies in the space and the flickering fireplace below the TV, it was hot in the room, and Sam had just done his best clenched-fist-to-the-heart belting vocal performance, which meant sweat was trickling down his temple and the small of his back. He didn't mind though. He was a performer, so even though it was living room karaoke with a group of family members and close friends, it had been worth all the sweat and strain on his vocal cords to put on a good show. Plus, he wasn't the only entertainer in the house, and he had to stay sharp, or Harlow would one-up him like she had time and time again back in LA at the cafe's open mic nights. He didn't actually mind that her vocal talent outshone his, of course. He was an actor on a popular television show. She was a single mom struggling to make it in theater. He was one of her biggest fans, and she seemed to love a little friendly competition, so he always brought it.

The group's hoots and applause died down, and Sam grabbed a swig of water. "Who's up next?" He held the mic out in invitation, raising a brow at his brothers—Matt first, then Clark, who were sitting beside one another on one end of the sofa, though he knew neither of them would indulge him. Matt smirked and shook his head. Clark scowled hard at Sam. Sam chuckled and glanced at Grayson and Finn, and it was clear they were out. Grayson was in an armchair, Finn on his lap, and they were whispering and nuzzling one another in a way that had Sam mentally storing the image to revisit later. He imagined the sweetness between the men translated into some very generous lovemaking. Realizing he was being a creeper, Sam looked to his sister and her... boyfriend and girlfriend. He was still processing that. But seeing them sitting together, Mara and Harlow beside one another on the sofa, Tyson seated on the floor in front of them, leaning on one shin of each woman, all of them smiling and chatting among themselves, just reinforced the "rightness" of their nontraditional relationship. None of them seemed eager to jump up and grab the mic. Dan, Hicks, and Wilkinson were milling around near the floor-to-ceiling windows, scowly-faced and straight-postured, discussing something that was no doubt very serious. That left...Bowen and Wyatt.

Sam looked back to the dining table, where he saw Bowen making little sandwiches of meat, cheese, and crackers to eat while he chatted with Wyatt, who was seated at the far end of the table. He was placed so he could see the living room where the karaoke was happening, but he was set apart from it at the far end of the long table. And he was...

Sam lifted the mic to his mouth, unaware that he'd even done so, and said, "Are you doing a puzzle?"

Wyatt's head snapped up, wide-eyed. Even from where Sam was standing, he saw his cheeks flush. Sam set the microphone down and cringed. He hoped someone would pick it up and start singing so that the attention he'd accidentally put on Wyatt would be placed on someone else. He really hadn't meant to embarrass Wyatt. He was just curious. Sam had never seen Wyatt do a puzzle before, but then again, there was a lot about Wyatt that was different now. But thinking about it, it did seem like a very "Wyatt" thing to do—sit in the next room with a jigsaw puzzle while the rest of the group got loud and rowdy. Wyatt was never judgmental about it; he just didn't like to be in the middle of the action. Very much the opposite of Sam, who lived for the spotlight.

Sam wove through the furniture of the great room and into the dining area. Bowen gave him a quick look before throwing stacks of the cheese, crackers, and salami on his plate and heading for the living room. "Who's got next?" he called loudly. "If no one takes it, I'm going to do my Ariana Grande..." There were groans and protestations from the living room, and Sam silently thanked Bowen for giving him and Wyatt some privacy.

Sam pulled out the chair to Wyatt's left and sat down. "Sorry about that," he said. "Didn't mean to call you out on the mic."

Wyatt didn't look at him, his eyes focused on the pieces in front of him, nimble fingers seizing a specific piece, turning it around, then placing it in its proper spot. "It's okay," he said.

Sam picked up the lid for the puzzle, smiling at the picture. It was a geometric pattern in rainbow colors. He knew Wyatt loved geometry—the way it "made sense" as Wyatt would say, was soothing to him. "So, you do puzzles now?"

Wyatt was picking up pieces, one by one, and trying them in a spot that was apparently giving him some difficulty. Sam thought he was really cute with his brows pulled in as he concentrated. "Yeah," Wyatt said. "My therapist suggested it. Said it might help with some of my anxiety." The piece in his hand clicked into place, and Wyatt's lips curved up in a tiny smile of triumph. Sam's heart squeezed. "Like the running," Wyatt added. He'd paused his puzzling to finally look at Sam. "And I really enjoy it," he said.

In the other room, Tyson and Harlow were singing a Taylor Swift and Zayn duet, and while it sounded pretty damn entertaining, Sam didn't have any desire to move from the spot he was in. "That's awesome," Sam said.

"It's nerdy."

Sam grinned. "Yes, but still awesome. Just like you," he said.

"Nerdy but still awesome?" Wyatt raised a brow.

"Exactly," Sam said.

They held one another's gaze, and Sam felt warmth swirl in his insides. "Do you ever let anyone puzzle with you?" he asked.

Wyatt took a beat before answering. "I didn't think anyone would want to." He dipped his head to start searching his pieces again.

Sam felt his eyes sting. "I'd want to, if you'd let me," he said softly.

Wyatt didn't look back up at him, but he said, "I put the

blues over there," and he nodded in Sam's direction. "If you want to work on those."

Sam couldn't help but smile as he got to work on the blue section of the puzzle. In the background, he could hear Mara take up the mic to sing some Alicia Keys, and while Sam would normally love to watch his sister—who lacked any speck of musical ability—butcher a beloved pop song, he had no intention of getting up from the table. If he was honest, based on the fluttering in his belly and the warmth in his cheeks, working on a jigsaw puzzle with Wyatt was the most fun he'd had since he could remember. It just felt good to be next to him. Even if they weren't talking. Sam imagined that this was what it would be like being Wyatt's partner. Living together, they'd probably have a designated puzzle station where they could work on puzzles and watch bad reality TV and simply relax. Sam had always found Wyatt's presence soothing, and the more famous he became, the more he craved the calm Wyatt brought him. But more than that, Sam thought about what he could be for Wyatt. Someone he could always be himself with. Someone who would never judge him for feeling anxious. Someone who would cherish him every single day that he was fortunate enough to be in his presence. Not for the first time over the last year, Sam mentally kicked himself for screwing things up with Wyatt when it seemed, at least for a brief moment, that he might have had a chance to prove to him how much they were truly meant to be.

"What are you thinking about?" Wyatt's question caught Sam a bit off guard. Wyatt hadn't looked up from the pieces he was placing much more quickly than Sam was.

"Oh," Sam said, unsure how much to reveal. The moment seemed so tentative he didn't want to say the wrong thing and shatter it. "Just thinking that it would be cool to have a designated puzzle area back home."

Wyatt looked up at him and raised a brow. "You put three pieces in the puzzle, and you want to commit to a puzzle station in your house?"

Sam grinned. "Maybe."

"And that piece doesn't actually go there," Wyatt said, pointing to the last piece Sam had placed.

"What?" Sam looked at the piece, incredulous. "It does!"

Wyatt shook his head. "No, it doesn't. I can see a little gap right here," he said, his finger tracing the spot where the piece didn't quite fit flush against its neighbor.

"Dammit," Sam mumbled, removing the piece. "So, I guess I got two pieces."

Wyatt's lips curled into a small smile. "The blues are hard, though," he said.

That was when Clark wandered into the dining room, pulling out a chair and sitting across the table from Sam to Wyatt's right. "Don't let Sam fuck up your puzzle," he said to Wyatt.

"Hey!" Sam said. "I got two pieces."

Wyatt and Clark exchanged a look. Sam scowled at his brother. Clark was the sibling Sam was closest to. He'd always been the one to look out for him the most and to be his voice of reason when he'd needed it. Because Clark was married to Bowen, who was Wyatt's uncle, he was also close to Wyatt. So, he'd been privy to the disintegration of their friendship the previous year. The expression on his face as he looked from Sam to Wyatt and back to Sam was assessing. Judging. Sam couldn't be sure, if it came down to it, whether Clark would even support Wyatt giving him a chance romantically or not. Clark was a bulldog, and he didn't want to see Sam nor Wyatt hurt. Clark spoke to Wyatt. "I'm going to need you to remind Bowen that the officiant is not the 'star' of the wedding."

Wyatt looked at Clark and nodded. "I know. I'll remind him. He was saying something about 'winging' the ceremony, and I was honestly a little concerned."

Clark rolled his eyes. "Yeah, I talked him into following a guideline from the internet. But that doesn't mean he won't pull a Bowen and add his own spice to it."

"I'll talk to him again," Wyatt said.

"Thanks," Clark said. "Sometimes I think he does the opposite of whatever I say, so I don't dare push it." Clark glanced into the living room with a fond look on his face for his husband.

"He'll stay in line," Wyatt said. "He won't want to mess it up for Matt."

Clark nodded. "I think you're right."

"So, is this what you two do?" Sam asked. "Tag team babysitting Bowen? Try to minimize the damage he leaves in his wake?"

Clark and Wyatt both nodded the affirmative. "Pretty much," Clark said, his smile for his man widening as Bowen blew him a kiss from across the space.

Clark eyed the progress they—mainly Wyatt—made on the puzzle. "So, you ready for the big race?" Clark asked.

Wyatt nodded. "I think so."

"What big race?" Sam hadn't heard anything about a race. Sure, he knew Wyatt ran regularly now. He was a runner. But a race was news to him.

Clark glared at Sam. "The half-marathon, jackass," he said, as if Sam was the greatest imbecile Clark had ever encountered.

"What half-marathon?" Sam looked to Wyatt, who

didn't look up from the puzzle. From the living room, Tyson was crooning along with Usher, and from the hoots and hollers from Matt, Jasper, Harlow, and Mara, he was dancing Usher-style, too.

"The Los Angeles Half-Marathon," Wyatt said simply.

"You're running it?"

"Of course he's running it," Clark said, still seemingly annoyed with Sam's obliviousness. "Why do you think he's been running at the crack of dawn on vacation?"

"Oh," Sam said. He looked at Wyatt. "That's amazing, though. Good for you. I'm sure you'll kill it."

"I don't know about that," Wyatt said. "But I think I'll finish."

Bowen came up behind Clark, bending to wrap his arms around Clark's neck and smack a kiss to his cheek. "We Prices always finish," he said to Sam with a wink. "Speaking of," he said more quietly to Clark. "Let's go to bed, babe."

A smile spread over Clark's face as he leaned into Bowen. "You don't have to ask me twice," he said. Bowen released him, Clark hopped up, and Sam watched them eagerly scamper out of the dining room and down the hall.

"They're still like a couple of teenagers," Sam commented to Wyatt. Wyatt smiled down at the puzzle pieces.

"Yeah," he said. "It's sweet. I'm happy for them."

Sam eyed him for a long moment. "Yeah," he said finally. "Me too."

And if that happiness was tinged with sharp jealousy for the type of close, loving relationship that Sam wanted with Wyatt, he wasn't going to dwell on that. He also wasn't going to dwell on the fact that Wyatt was going to run a half-marathon and hadn't bothered to tell him. No one had.

Not for the first time since arriving in Vail, Sam was hit with a reminder of just how much had changed between him and Wyatt. And deep in his bones, he felt the need to rectify that. He wanted to be a part of his life. He wanted to not only know about the big things, he wanted to be right by Wyatt's side as he did them.

"Hey, Wyatt?" Sam's voice was tentative, and nerves churned in his belly.

"Yeah?" Wyatt looked up at him, halting his quest for the next orange piece.

"Can I come to the race? To cheer you on?"

Wyatt looked at him with what looked to Sam like confusion for a few seconds. Then Wyatt said, "You don't have to do that."

Sam shook his head. "I want to. If you'll let me."

Wyatt's Adam's apple bobbed as he swallowed, and Sam was dying to know what he was thinking in that moment. Had he crossed a line? Had he pushed too hard? Was Wyatt thinking of the best way to tell him to kindly fuck off?

Finally, Wyatt said, "Okay."

Sam let out a breath and grinned at him. "Great," he said. "I'll make some signs for me and Dan-o to hold up along the route."

A slight look of panic widened Wyatt's eyes, and he shook his head. "No, that's not necessary. Danson won't want to hold a sign."

Sam continued to grin at Wyatt. "Maybe not. But he will."

# Chapter Ten

## Wyatt

Wyatt was alone, tucked into his side of the bed he shared with Sam, staring up at the ceiling. He'd gone to bed over an hour ago, but he hadn't been able to sleep. He tried to tell himself it was because he could hear the distant voices of the remaining members of the group still up chatting and laughing in the great room, but he knew that wasn't truly the reason. He rolled onto his side and faced the wall, pulling the covers up further as if snuggling in deeper could somehow clear his mind. It had been a crazy twenty-four hours. It had gone from the insanity of him presenting himself to Sam in his underwear the day before to the moment a few hours earlier when he'd nearly burst into tears when Sam had said he'd come to his half-marathon. Wyatt's emotions had been all over the place, and even working on his puzzle hadn't been able to calm him. Hell, he'd been two seconds away from suggesting that he and Sam move in together, make a puzzle station, and get married. Like that line of crazy thinking wouldn't have sent Sam running again. Thankfully, he'd held back the wild fantasy of happy domestic life with Sam, rolled up his puzzle, and gone to bed.

When Wyatt heard Sam and Danson talking in the hallway a few minutes later, he closed his eyes and concentrated on evening out his breathing. He wasn't entirely sure why, but when Sam opened the door, Wyatt pretended to be asleep. Mainly, he suspected, it was his instinct to avoid talking with Sam because if he did, he might end up saying something stupid and embarrassing that he couldn't take back. And, shit. He'd forgotten to focus on even breaths in and out. He willed his heart to slow down as he heard the sound of Sam lowering his zipper, kicking out of his jeans, pulling his shirt over his head, and tossing it to the floor. Wyatt swallowed, the sound of it loud in his own ears. He held perfectly still as Sam lifted the covers and slid into bed, plopping his head on the pillow with a sigh. For a few long seconds, Wyatt thought he had Sam fooled, but then Sam spoke.

"I know you're awake."

Wyatt didn't even bother keeping up the pretense. "How'd you know?" He rolled onto his back, mimicking Sam's position, heads on pillows, eyes on the ceiling, hands resting at their sides. It should have felt much more awkward than it did. But Wyatt couldn't help but recognize that no matter how much was unsaid between them, or how much water had yet to flow under the bridge, he always felt right in Sam's presence. Like there was something about Sam that soothed him. Sure, being near Sam made him nervous, but that had always been the case. First it was because he was so attracted to him. Then it had been because he was secretly in love with him. Now, it was because that secret lay open between them with nowhere to hide. And Wyatt had to live with the uncomfortable reality of being in close proximity to someone who didn't love him back. That should have made him uncomfortable. Should have made it impossible to share a space with him. But somehow, despite everything, Sam's presence eased something deep inside Wyatt. Like Sam could really see who he was, and he accepted that. That was something Wyatt had never felt with anyone, apart from his Uncle Bowen. And finding that with someone he was also incredibly attracted to and had romantic feelings toward? It was potent. Always had been, and, Wyatt feared, always would be.

"I could practically hear you counting your inhales and exhales in your mind." Sam's voice sounded affectionate and tired. Wyatt wasn't sure what time it was, but he'd gone to bed around midnight, so it had to be the wee hours of the morning.

"You know me too well," Wyatt said. He could feel the slight shift as Sam turned onto his side. Wyatt could feel his eyes on him, even in the dark.

"You think so?" He sounded genuinely concerned about the answer. "Do I still know you?"

Wyatt shifted onto his side, too, so they were looking at one another. Through the blackness of the room, Wyatt could just make out Sam's form across the bed from him. He couldn't see his expression, but he felt it: intensity. He didn't know what type of intensity—where it came from or what it meant—but he could feel it plain as day. This was a serious question from Sam, and he needed an honest answer.

"Of course you do," Wyatt said softly.

"You've changed, though." Sam sounded resigned about that.

"For the better," Wyatt said. "The running. The

puzzles. I needed something to help me cope with...things. And they have."

"That's great," Sam said, still sounding discouraged.

"But I'm still me," Wyatt said. He didn't have time to think through his movement. He simply acted on instinct. Something about the hazy darkness of lying awake in the middle of the night weakened his compulsion to overanalyze everything he did before he did it. He extended his hand out into the space between them, sliding it over the smooth cotton sheet. He knew Sam wouldn't be able to see his gesture, but somehow, he knew that when he reached out, Sam's fingers would meet his. And they did. Sam placed his hand over Wyatt's and squeezed.

Wyatt was the one with the next question. It was something he'd wanted to know for a long time but had been too afraid and too hurt to ask.

"Do you miss Blair?"

Wyatt hated the thought that Sam might still be pining for his actress ex, and Blair was a sore subject for him overall. But he had to know. He had to.

"Well, we still work together," Sam said. His thumb slowly massaged Wyatt's wrist, and his skin prickled at his touch. It was somehow comforting and electrifying. But that pretty much summarized how being with Sam had always felt.

"You know what I mean," Wyatt said, not wanting to be deterred.

"No," Sam said firmly. "We weren't right together."

That felt both reassuring and unsettling. If Sam had not wanted to be with him because he'd loved Blair more, and Blair wasn't right for him, then where did that leave Wyatt? Somewhere on his D-list of acquaintances? Wyatt knew his thoughts were dramatic, but he couldn't help himself.

"Oh," he said, simply, trying to draw his hand away, but Sam snatched it and squeezed harder.

"That's it," Sam said, tugging a little on Wyatt's hand to pull him closer. Wyatt could feel the tension in Sam's body where he held Wyatt in place next to him. "You listen to me, Wyatt Price."

Wyatt froze. He hadn't heard this particular type of agitation from Sam in a long time. And he knew better than to do anything but keep his mouth shut and listen to whatever it was Sam wanted to say.

"That night..." Wyatt knew exactly what night he meant without any context. *The night.* The night they'd had their ugly fight. The night Sam and Blair had fought. Over him. Where Sam had said he loved Blair and not Wyatt...

"You misunderstood me. And you never let me explain. You wouldn't fucking listen to me, and I just gave up. And I'm sorry for that. I truly am. But you will listen to me now."

Wyatt nodded, though he wasn't sure Sam could see him. They were close enough where Wyatt could feel the heat of Sam's body and the tension radiating from him as he spoke.

"Blair asked me if I loved you like I loved her," Sam said, recapping one of the worst moments of Wyatt's life. "And I told her no."

"I re—"

"Don't you dare interrupt me this time, Wyatt." Sam's voice was firm, and Wyatt shut his mouth.

"I told her no because I didn't love you like I loved her. But I do love you. Differently. More."

Wyatt held his breath. He was caught up on the present tense of the word "do." Sam hadn't said, "I did love you." He'd said, "I do love you." Wyatt's heart thumped hard, and when his chest felt like it would burst, he let out a long, slow breath. He was never one to overlook a detail, and this one was important.

"Did you say do?" Wyatt's voice was cautious, not wanting to hope.

"What?" Sam didn't seem to understand the absolute urgency of clarifying that verb tense issue that very instant.

"You said, 'I do love you.'"

"Yes," Sam said.

"Did you mean 'I did love you'?"

"Yes," Sam said, and Wyatt's heart deflated. But then Sam continued. "Yes, I did love you. And I do love you. I will always love you. Not the way I loved Blair. Or the way I love anyone else on this earth, Wyatt. You're different and special and...more."

Wyatt flipped his hand so he could grab Sam's wrist, and he tugged him hard. Wyatt's mouth found Sam's just as effortlessly as their hands had joined. The pressure of Sam's full lips against his was delicious. He wriggled an arm around Sam's waist and held him close. Sam's warm tongue swept into Wyatt's mouth as he also curled an arm around Wyatt. The brush of their tongues tripped every switch in Wyatt's body, sparking him to life in a way he'd never imagined. If he'd been able to slow the swirling of his head long enough to think, he'd probably be worried he was in danger of cardiac arrest. His chest felt warm on the inside, his stomach fluttering. Lust tingled through him as he felt Sam wedge a knee between his legs. He couldn't help but moan and claw at Sam, feeling like his heart might actually burst from sensory overload and pure joy.

Sam kissed him hungrily. Like he'd been dying to kiss Wyatt as long as Wyatt had been dying to kiss him. Sam's hand had crept underneath the hem of Wyatt's T-shirt, his palm pressed firmly into the small of Wyatt's back, like he was afraid he'd get away if he let go.

Wyatt wasn't going anywhere. They kissed and touched and held each other in the way Wyatt had always dreamed they would. And if Wyatt could have possibly loved Sam any more than he already did, the unspoken understanding Sam had that Wyatt didn't want to go further—that he wanted to just enjoy this step, something they'd never done together before—would have made him fall even deeper. Sam's hands and mouth were curious, yet tender, and Wyatt luxuriated in the feel of Sam's hard, lean body against his. It was so much better than anything Wyatt could ever have imagined, that making out with Sam actually caused Wyatt to forget his worries. He wasn't anxious; he wasn't worrying about what it all meant. He wasn't afraid of the conversations they hadn't had yet, the words still unspoken, the wounds still unhealed. Instead, he just let himself feel. Warmth and excitement, lust and affection, elation and contentment. Everything he'd ever wanted was right there, in his arms, and Wyatt would not miss out on the experience. He just let himself feel.

At some point, Wyatt had fallen asleep half-sprawled over Sam's body, Sam's fingers gently playing with his hair. The last thing he remembered was kissing Sam's chest, right over his heart, and wrapping his arm around Sam's waist, holding on to the most perfect moment that he'd ever had.

# Chapter Eleven

## Sam

Because the last family member of Sam's to get married had been Clark, and he and Bowen had not bothered with all the pomp and circumstance of a big wedding, opting instead to elope in Vegas, Sam had never been to a wedding rehearsal, much less a rehearsal dinner. He didn't even really know what the point was—how hard was it to walk down an aisle and stand still for fifteen minutes? But apparently, it was a thing.

Winston the Wedding Planner, a very no-nonsense man in his early fifties, had met their group at the Aspen Wind Chalet, which was the restaurant and event space at the top of the mountain. *Yes. That's right. Matty and Jasper were going to have their wedding ceremony on the literal top of a mountain.* Sam never thought he'd see the day. He and his siblings had not had an easy go of it in their early life, and now his brother was marrying a millionaire on a fucking mountaintop. And he himself had a personal security professional as his plus-one. Weird. Speaking of whom, Sam looked on in amusement as he watched Dan-o speak heatedly with Winston the Wedding Planner. The last he'd heard, Winston objected to Dan, Wilkinson, and Hicks insisting on searching all the vendors' shipments and bags as they arrived at the venue. Winston was vehement that he only worked with the best of the best, and he could personally vouch for all the vendors. When Hicks had replied with, "I don't know you. I can't trust your judgment," Winston had gasped, a hand flying to his chest in affronted horror. Hicks had muttered something about not having time for this, and he and Wilkinson had stalked off to their next concern. Dan was left to deal with Winston, who had never, in his twenty-five years as Colorado's most sought-after wedding planner, had to deal with such disrespect. If Dan had trouble keeping his patience with Sam, he was no match for Winston. Sam just wished he had popcorn to watch their exchange.

"What's that about?" Wyatt stood next to Sam, his eyes on Dan and Winston.

"Dan's getting torn a new one by the wedding planner," Sam said, smiling at Wyatt. He couldn't help himself from inching closer so that their arms brushed. By unspoken agreement, they hadn't divulged what had happened between them the night before to anyone else. The two of them kissing would have been a big enough deal to rock the boat, and they both knew better than to do that on rehearsal dinner night. But that didn't mean Sam couldn't sneak a few touches here and there, especially if everyone else was otherwise occupied with the wedding preparations and excitement.

Wyatt smiled back, pressing his arm into Sam's in return. "It does look like Danson's met his match." Winston's hands were on his hips then, his body leaning forward into Dan's space, his face upturned to look Dan straight in the eye.

Sam really wanted to grab Wyatt's hand, to twine their fingers together, but he didn't dare. That probably wouldn't go unnoticed. He glanced around the mountaintop space, which served as sort of a tourist attraction. They'd rode gondolas up the mountain from the parking lot below. On the way up, they'd had incredible views of the endless expanse of sky rising from behind clusters of mountains, trees and clouds and snow-capped peaks in the distance. At the mountaintop, there were various attractions: an alpine slide at one end, a zip line at the other, and a massive, high-end restaurant/bar/event space in the center. Hiking paths connected everything and also meandered down the mountainside in long, zigzags of trampled rock. The ceremony was to take place outside, over-looking the Rockies. They'd already done the practice run-through of that, the wedding party walking down the aisle at a certain pace, finding their marks, and standing beside Jasper and Matt as they said their vows. Bowen hadn't actually gone through the content of the ceremony, for which Sam was grateful. He'd been hungry and ready to move on to the dinner phase of the evening. And that's where he found himself now. Waiting around for the dinner bell, so to speak, Dan and Winston his entertainment as he passed the time.

"Do you know how much longer until we eat?" Sam asked Wyatt.

Wyatt glanced at his smartwatch, which Winston the Wedding Planner had warned him not to wear to the actual wedding ceremony, telling him it was "tacky enough to ruin everything." Sam had barked a laugh at that, which had earned him a deadly glare from Winston that snapped him back into line. "About ten minutes," Wyatt said. He blew out a long breath, and Sam noted him drumming his fingers on his thighs.

"You okay?" Sam rounded on Wyatt to take him in properly.

Wyatt shrugged. "Yeah, I'm fine," he said. But Sam could see him doing that thing where he counted his breaths on the way in, held his breath for a few beats, then let it out slowly. A telltale sign that he was anxious and trying to work himself back down.

"Come on," Sam said, not giving a fuck anymore about what anyone thought, and took Wyatt's hand. "Walk with me."

Wyatt glanced around them, like he was nervous someone would see them walk off together, but everyone else was occupied in their own conversations or taking photos of the view in the setting sunlight. He threaded his fingers through Sam's and held on tightly, nodding. "Okay," he said.

Sam led him toward the front of the restaurant building, where the gondolas had dropped them off. The views were on the back side, so they'd have more privacy going around front. Hand in hand, they slowly trod one of the dirt paths leading down the mountainside. "Talk to me," Sam said. "You're freaking out about something." Sam really hoped it wasn't about what had happened between them. Because Wyatt regretting the best night of Sam's life would gut him. He didn't want Wyatt to be unsettled about anything, but him pulling away from Sam again now that they'd finally started connecting would be devastating.

Wyatt squeezed his hand a bit tighter, and Sam wasn't sure whether it was to help steady his feet or his troubled mind. Either way, Sam hoped he could give him the support he needed. "I am freaking out a little," Wyatt said.

"Why?" Sam again silently hoped that it wasn't about their kiss. He would give anything—anything at all—for Wyatt not to regret it.

"It's just..." Wyatt trailed off, and Sam came to a halt beside an ancient aspen. He faced Wyatt, holding his hand tightly, and patiently waited for Wyatt to gather his thoughts. Wyatt looked him in the eye, and Sam's heart jumped. He was beautiful in the golden-hour light, looking at Sam like he was holding his guard up by a thread. Like he was waging war with himself on whether to be vulnerable and let Sam in. Sam held his own breath while Wyatt's internal battle played out. Finally, Wyatt seemed to come to a decision. He held Sam's gaze. "It's just all these people. And I'm afraid that Bowen will be able to tell something happened between us, and then he'll blurt it out to everyone, and I don't want everyone paying attention to me. And I'm still trying to process things myself. I don't need to add Uncle Bo, and your siblings, and Grayson Fucking Winter into the mix."

Sam fought hard not to smile. He felt for Wyatt, but he was so damn adorable that it was impossible not to find it charming. "You're embarrassed that Grayson Winter might find out that you made out with me last night?" Wyatt's expression was troubled, and Sam was sure it was soon going to be angry, as well, if he didn't tread carefully. Sam went on, "Is it because he was your OG celebrity crush and if he knows you kissed me, you fear you no longer have a chance with him?"

Wyatt's eyes flew wide. "What? No!"

Sam's lips curved up, and Wyatt's expression morphed from confusion to annoyance. "You're making fun of me."

Sam nodded. "Little bit."

"I'm trying to confess my worries, here," Wyatt said,

"pour my heart out, and you're laughing at me." Sam noted that Wyatt was still grasping his hand firmly, and that to Sam's trained observation skills, a hint of a smile could be detected right beneath the surface of Wyatt's facade of affrontedness.

"So, what you're telling me," Sam continued, rubbing his thumb along the back of Wyatt's hand as he held on to it, "is that you're so affected by making out with me that you're afraid people can see the profound impact I made all over you?"

Wyatt narrowed his eyes at Sam. "You are infuriating."

"It was a good kiss," Sam said. "I don't blame you if it changed your life." He said the words as a joke, but he was well aware of their real significance. Kissing Wyatt had been life changing for him. It was something he'd wanted for so long, and it exceeded all the fantasies he'd ever had about the moment. A warm rush of extreme "rightness" had taken over Sam's body when they'd finally taken that step. A step he knew would alter him. Sam knew without a doubt that his life would forever be divided in his mind into before and after he'd come to his senses and kissed Wyatt Price.

"Worse than infuriating," Wyatt said, hazel eyes intense. "You're absolutely insufferable," he said, voice sounding thicker with emotion than it had a moment before. Maybe there was some desire in there, too.

Sam brought his other hand to Wyatt's arm, sliding it down his forearm slowly before twining their free hands together. They stood there, below the aspen on the mountain trail, the setting sun flooding them with golden-pink light, facing one another, holding both hands. Sam briefly recalled the image of Matt and Jasper standing in the same exact position in front of their rustic altar an hour earlier during the rehearsal. "But you still love me," Sam said softly, his heart hammering in his chest.

"True," Wyatt said, his voice a whisper.

"And you want to kiss me again," Sam said.

"Also true," Wyatt agreed.

Sam gently tugged on both of Wyatt's hands, bringing him in closer until he could rest his forehead against Wyatt's. "I love you too," Sam murmured before pressing his lips to Wyatt's in the softest, most significant kiss of his life.

Wyatt's lips pressed back, and Sam wrapped their joined hands around Wyatt's back, enveloping him as he deepened the kiss.

A few seconds later, breathless and more than a little turned on, Wyatt pulled away from Sam, worry back on his face. "What is it?" The nerves immediately fluttered back into Sam's belly at Wyatt's furrowed brow and the way his posture had stiffened slightly again. "What's wrong?"

"It's so stupid," Wyatt said.

"What's stupid?" Sam needed Wyatt to start explaining himself so that Sam could ease whatever worries he was having and start kissing him again.

"I just keep thinking about what might happen if we keep...you know..."

Sam nodded. It was a lot to think about, and they'd barely begun to discuss the implications of them finally getting together. If that's what was happening. And Sam knew he had a lot of apologizing yet to do for the way he'd left things with Wyatt last year. "Wyatt," Sam started. "I promise I'll prove to you how sorry I am..."

Wyatt shook his head, seemingly frustrated. "I don't mean that. Not the emotional stuff. I mean, of course I know we need to talk about that, but I was more thinking about the...physical part?"

Sam took a second to put together the pieces, and when he did, his smile was likely smugger than Bowen's after he and Clark emerged from their room following a midday "nap." "Are you talking about sex?"

Wyatt looked away, and Sam could see him blush up to the tips of his ears. "Maybe."

"You're worried about having sex with me?" Sam tried not to tease him. He was fucking stoked that Wyatt was thinking about having sex with him, but he also wanted to respect whatever was troubling him about it.

"It's not that," Wyatt said. He peeked up at Sam and mumbled the next part. "I'm just weird about safety and stuff. And I haven't actually been with anyone in like...all the ways. And I know you've...you know. So I really want to do...stuff with you—all the things, really—but I just want to make sure we're safe to..."

Sam let out a breath of relief. While Wyatt's safe-sex concerns were legitimate, Sam was relieved that was all he was worried about. "First of all, you are so adorable, even when trying to politely ask me if I have gonorrhea. Secondly, I am completely STI free," Sam told him. "After Blair, I got the whole workup. I could log into the app thing to show you, if you'd like?"

Wyatt looked him in the eye. "If you say you've been tested, I trust you."

"I'll show you the tests in the app anyway," Sam said. "Just for peace of mind." Wyatt smiled then, and Sam felt light and warm and beyond excited. "But, just to be clear," Sam said, fighting to keep his tone neutral. "You are saying you want to have all the sex with me?" When Wyatt bit his lip and looked at their feet, Sam wanted to break out into a jig. But he didn't. At least not outwardly.

"Maybe," Wyatt said. "I was considering all the possibilities." Sam tugged him in for a more than suggestive kiss.

"And what's the verdict now?"

"Probable."

"I'll take it." Sam kissed Wyatt again, hoping to improve his chances even more.

# Chapter Twelve

## Wyatt

"Remember the time we were watching Sam's pilot and Wyatt got all drunk?" Mara was laughing as she posed the question to their table at the rehearsal dinner. "That was so funny. Wyatt, you were hilarious."

Wyatt tried to smile, though he felt his cheeks heat in embarrassment at the memory. He didn't blame Mara for bringing it up. To her, it was a funny anecdote. She didn't realize that had been at the peak of Wyatt's struggle with his initial discovery of feelings for Sam, who at that point had been his best friend. He wasn't sure how their table had gotten started down the retelling drunken shenanigans from the past road, but there they were, and Wyatt was not especially pleased to be there.

"I remember," Wyatt managed. He didn't want to relive the memory of getting sloppy drunk and lamenting that Sam's costar got to kiss Sam. It had been mortifying.

"I remember Bowen ripping Clark a new one over letting Wyatt get drunk on his watch," Sam cut in, placing a hand on Wyatt's knee under the table and squeezing. Wyatt was thankful that Sam had shifted the focus of the conversation off him.

"That's right!" Mara grinned. "And then they got it on in the next room while we were all still trying to watch the episode."

"Did not," Clark protested. "There may have been some physical contact during our...conversation...but we did not get it on."

"If you say so," Mara said, taking a healthy swig of her wine.

"So, you all knew each other before Sam was famous?" Tyson, who was bouncing Milo on his knee, asked the group, eyes mainly on Wyatt, since the majority of the table was the Deerwood siblings. Wyatt assumed by "you all" he meant Wyatt and Bowen knowing the Deerwoods.

"Yeah," Wyatt said. "Uncle Bo went into business with Matty first. Then he met Clark, and we all just..."

"Became one big happy family," Mara finished for him, speaking the words in a high-pitched voice as she tickled Milo's tummy.

"That's really cool," Harlow said from the seat on Tyson's other side.

"It's something, alright," Clark muttered. Wyatt could tell he was wearing his scowl of fondness, though. Clark was a grump, and he had a perma-scowl, but he loved his siblings, whether he wanted to express that openly or not. That was part of why Wyatt liked him so much as his step-uncle. He was one of the only people Wyatt had ever met who could match his Uncle Bo in his capacity to love and support his family. They'd really hit the jackpot with the whole family, though Mara was doing her level best to piss Wyatt off at the moment with the drunk Wyatt stories. But if a tipsy Mara was the biggest hiccup in the rehearsal, that was pretty good.

Matt and Jasper had made some speeches before the meal, thanking everyone for being part of their special day. Then Hicks had taken the mic to give a few gruff reminders about security, and then they could eat. Wyatt was a little shocked at the elaborate spread of food and beverages available, considering this was the rehearsal dinner and not the main event, but then he knew that Jasper was known to appreciate the finer things in life, no matter how inconsequential his groom found them. Wyatt thought that what made Matt and Jasper work so well as a couple was that balance. Some might say they were too different to be compatible, but Wyatt didn't see it that way. They were the counterpart to one another, each bringing something to the relationship that the other didn't quite possess on his own. To Wyatt, it was a beautiful thing.

Wyatt slid his entree plate away from him, leaving only a few bites of asparagus on the plate. The food had been delicious, and they'd rehearsed until the cows had come home. So Wyatt just wanted them to be done so he could go back to the lodge and put on his pajamas. It had been a lot of socializing for one day. He felt his cheeks heat a bit at the thought he then had about wanting Sam in bed with him while he wore said pajamas, preferably about to take them off. Wyatt cleared his throat and took a sip of ice water from the half-empty goblet in front of him. Best not to go there while he was sitting with a table of Sam's siblings.

When it sounded like Mara was going to start in on another story, Wyatt decided he might need more than a sip of water to settle himself. What he needed was a break. "I'm gonna use the restroom," Wyatt said quietly, standing and excusing himself. It wasn't that he was so bothered by the conversation. It was more that the day had just been very long, and he'd done way more people-ing than he preferred.

He had half expected Sam to get up and follow him, but he was slightly relieved he hadn't. With everything that had happened between them the night before, he was understandably overwhelmed with emotion. It was good emotion, elation, in fact, that he and Sam had finally kissed, and Sam had told him he loved him. But there was also fear. It seemed like he was getting everything he'd wanted all those months ago when he'd originally told Sam how he felt. But nothing had changed between them. So why was Sam acting so differently now? And could Wyatt dare to trust it? Of course, with the full lodge of people and the rehearsal, he and Sam hadn't had any alone time to talk things through. Add that to having to be social all day and well into the evening already, and it was...a lot. Wyatt just needed a few minutes to himself to breathe.

He used the bathroom, took his time washing his hands, and stared at himself in the mirror. He'd pulled his hair back with a black hair tie, and he wore one of his standard black business suits. He'd had to buy a new belt to accommodate his trimmer waist since he'd taken up running. He'd always been slim, but now his body was even more streamlined, muscles popping up in his legs, a firmer ass, and a narrower waist. He thought he looked pretty good, if he was honest. He'd never been one to have an overabundance of confidence. That was something he hadn't inherited from his Uncle Bo, unfortunately. But checking out his reflection, even Wyatt could admit he cleaned up okay.

Looking at his reflection reminded him that Sam's hands had been all over his body the night before. He'd run his palms over Wyatt's waist, slid them up his back, squeezed his biceps. It had felt better than anything Wyatt had ever experienced. People seemed to believe that "sex was sex," but Wyatt begged to differ. Just making out with the man he loved had been more erotic for him than any sexual encounter he'd ever had. Not that there was an over-abundance of them to begin with, but to borrow Sam's words to him, it was different, and special, and more.

But was it real? How long would he have it? Was it just the convenience of rooming together that had Sam singing a different tune about their relationship? Was it because things had fizzled out with Blair? Did Sam really mean what he'd said? Wyatt wished he could just believe it. He wanted to so badly. But he'd been hurt before, and he had to keep at least some semblance of a guard in place.

He took a deep breath in the mirror and let it out slowly. He wasn't going to sabotage this if it was real. If there was the possibility that something was finally happening between him and Sam, he wasn't going to be too big of a coward to at least pursue it. He knew full well the odds weren't foolproof. He could possibly get hurt again. Even worse this time now that they'd progressed to the physical part. But he had to try. Because it was Sam.

The entree plates had been cleared from the table when he returned, and the venue's caterers were bustling around with coffee service and dessert. There was still probably a good hour left of this rehearsal dinner business. Wyatt worked hard to have a calm, cool expression on his face as he pulled out his chair to sit and rejoin the table. Harlow and Mara were bickering with Clark about something related to Clark's theater. It sounded like Harlow was going to star in another of Clark's productions and took issue with one of the scenes. Clark dug his heels in and said he was the director, and therefore, it was his decision. Tyson loudly proclaimed that he was "staying out of it," and both Mara and Harlow looked ready to attack.

Wyatt took a sip from his water goblet as a server came around with the coffee and plates of caramel cheesecake. "Here," Sam said, quietly enough for just Wyatt to hear. He slid his cell phone in front of Wyatt beside his cheesecake plate.

"What's this for?" Wyatt asked, looking blankly at the phone and then up at Sam.

Sam reached over and tapped the phone, the screen lighting up. "Thought you might..." He trailed off, and Wyatt pulled the phone closer, looking at the screen. It was an app of some sort that Wyatt didn't recognize, but after a few seconds he registered what he was looking at.

"It's a puzzle app?" He looked over at Sam, and Wyatt could feel a grateful smile curving his lips.

"Yeah," Sam said. "And you can upload your own photos, and the app turns them into a puzzle. Here. Look," Sam said, dragging one of the pieces to the left corner of the puzzle grid space. "This might give you a hint."

Wyatt immediately recognized the sign for Bowen and Matt's cafe, and a quick glance at the other pieces on the screen told him what image Sam had selected. "This is us when the cafe opened," he said. "When Mara insisted that you and I would 'look pretty together' for the social media post she was making." Wyatt smiled at the memory of Sam slinging an arm around his shoulder as he'd agreed whole-heartedly with Mara that they did, indeed, look damn good together. Wyatt had been uneasy and awkward, but he'd smiled for the photo. It had been impossible not to smile with Sam's arm around him.

"Yeah," Sam said. "Anyway, if you're overwhelmed or

whatever, I figured you might like a puzzle." He shrugged like it was no big deal.

"Thank you," Wyatt said, picking up the phone and focusing on the pieces. He didn't dare keep looking at Sam. He didn't want to let on just how big a deal this little gesture really was for him.

"Anytime," Sam said softly, and another piece of Wyatt's heart surrendered to Sam's claim.

# Chapter Thirteen

## Sam

"Big Dan," Sam said, using all the charm he could muster. "It's just a walk around the lodge. I swear I'll stay within eyesight of the house at all times."

"I'll go with you," Dan said firmly.

"I wasn't planning on going alone," Sam said. "But you weren't my companion of choice. No offense."

Dan's expression didn't change. He looked at Sam with resolve and his patented "I'm not amused by your antics" expression.

"Take whoever you want, but I'm going with you. It's my job."

Sam pouted but nodded. *Fine.* If Dan wanted to play third wheel on his romantic moonlit stroll with Wyatt, so be it. They'd been back from the rehearsal dinner for a few minutes, everyone bustling around the lodge, changing into sweats, cracking beers, and talking loudly about the next day's main event. Matt and Jasper had gone to bed early, no doubt nervous and excited. Sam wondered if Matty had written his own vows, and he had a hard time imagining that. Matt was an emotional guy, no doubt, but he usually kept those emotions private. Apparently, he shared them with Jasper, though, which Sam found endlessly adorable. Jasper was Sam's boss—the bigwig showrunner of *Ominous* —but he was also an endlessly sweet man when it came to Matt. From the outside looking in, Matt and Jasper were a bit of an odd couple, but Sam knew better. Despite their differences, they worked.

Sam, followed closely by Dan, wandered into the lodge's great room, looking for Wyatt. After the rehearsal, Matt's best man, Ethan, and Ethan's husband, Felix, had come back to the lodge to hang out with Grayson and Finn. Ethan and Felix were "normals"—at least in terms of not needing their own personal security officer, but they both worked in show business. Ethan was a writer on Grayson and Finn's show, and Felix was a personal trainer. He worked with most of the celebrities who'd be present at the wedding, in fact. The newcomers, along with Grayson, Finn, Clark, and Bowen were gathered around the dining table, drinking and laughing. A lot of people would pay a pretty penny for a candid photo of that collected group, and Sam had a slight moment of guilt for giving Dan a hard time. The personal security officers did have a tough job, tirelessly working to ensure the safety as well as the privacy of their celebrity clients. The only reason people like Grayson and Finn could live any sort of normal life was because of people like Hicks, Wilkinson, and Dan.

Sam found Wyatt in an armchair in the corner of the living room, typing away on his phone. "Hey," Sam said, sitting down on the coffee table and facing Wyatt. Wyatt's thumbs continued to swiftly tap for a few moments before stopping. Wyatt looked up at Sam, a warmth in his expression giving Sam the stomach butterflies he had started to think of as "The Wyatt Effect." Even when Sam had been in serious relationships, including the one with Blair, no one had given him the flutters the way Wyatt did. He should have known that meant something. He knew it now.

"Hey," Wyatt said. "You changed quickly," he added, nodding to Sam's black sweats and hoodie.

"Yeah," Sam said. "When I'm not on set in costume and required to look cool, I refuse to wear anything with zippers or buttons. It makes no sense to me."

Wyatt shook his head in amusement, then pinched the fabric of the dress shirt he was still wearing. "I pretty much live in a shirt and tie. Unless I'm running," he added.

"I know," Sam said. "I remember the first day I met you. I was so disappointed you didn't pull out an actual pocket protector."

Wyatt's brows drew in, a look of confusion crossing his face. "Of course I didn't. How can it properly protect my pocket if I'm pulling it out willy-nilly?"

Sam barked out a laugh, and Wyatt grinned at him.

"So, I was thinking," Sam said as their laughter died down. "That you might want to go for a walk with me?"

Wyatt glanced out the windows, noting the blackness of the sky that was customary at such an hour. "Now?"

"Yeah," Sam nodded. "Grab your coat. It's not too cold." Sam cocked his head slightly, indicating the place where Dan stood by the fireplace, failing to look like he was casually standing there and not babysitting Sam. "And Dan-o will be trailing us, just in case you didn't want to venture out with me unchaperoned." He raised his brows at Wyatt suggestively, and Wyatt rolled his eyes.

"Okay," Wyatt said, standing up from the chair. "I'll grab my coat."

"Wow," Wyatt said a few minutes later, his head tilted

all the way back to look at the sky. "We do not have stars like this in Los Angeles."

"I know, right?" Sam stood beside him, taking his hand. Wyatt laced his fingers through Sam's, holding tight. Sam immediately felt warmer, and he squeezed Wyatt's hand lightly just to feel that he was really there with him.

They'd walked around the lodge's grounds, making their way to the front of the house—the side that faced the mountains rather than the road—and ended up near a copse of pines that grew at the edge of the property. They hadn't spoken much, just admired the crisp, clear night and the beauty of the stars, which glittered more vibrantly than either of them had ever really imagined possible. Sure, they'd been to Colorado on vacation before, but they'd never looked up at the stars quite like this: from a mountain lodge, surrounded by family and friends, side by side, together. Hand in hand with Wyatt, Sam saw the world differently. It was vaster, brimming with more wonder and beauty and possibility than he could have possibly fathomed on his own. It didn't quite feel real. The Wyatt Effect made everything seem a little like magic. And coming from someone who played a wizard on a television show for a living, the power of that wasn't lost on Sam.

After a few minutes of silence, in which Sam's mind was whirring with questions and hopes about what all this with Wyatt meant, Wyatt spoke. "Sam?" His voice sounded tentative, like he was nervous about whatever he was about to say.

"Yeah?" Sam squeezed Wyatt's hand lightly in encouragement.

"Has something..." Wyatt trailed off, as if discarding what he was about to say and rethinking it. "Have you..."

"What?" Sam asked. "You can ask me anything."

Wyatt looked up at the stars again, as if gathering strength from them. "Okay," he said, letting out a slow breath. "I'm just going to ask..."

Sam waited, not wanting to interrupt, but he held firm to Wyatt's hand.

"Did you mean it?" Wyatt's eyes were on Sam then, and even through the darkness, Sam could feel their intensity. He knew that whatever he said to Wyatt in that moment was important and needed to be truthful. He had no problem with that.

"Did I mean what?" He had a pretty good idea, but it never hurt to clarify.

"What you said last night," Wyatt said. "That you...you know..."

Sam squeezed Wyatt's hand. He'd wanted to simply pull him in and squeeze some sense into him, but he didn't want to do anything that might spook Wyatt. "When I said that I loved you?" Sam supplied.

"Yeah," Wyatt said. "That."

"Yes," Sam said. "Of course I meant it. I have always loved you, Wyatt. Please tell me you believe that."

Wyatt was quiet for painfully long moments, and Sam held his breath. Finally, his voice shaky and incredibly quiet, Wyatt said, "I'm scared to believe it."

Sam couldn't handle it any longer. He released Wyatt's hand long enough to wrap his arms around him and pull him into a tight embrace. He held Wyatt against him fiercely, and he felt Wyatt relax into him. Wyatt snaked his arms around Sam's waist and held him tight, too. Into Wyatt's neck, Sam whispered, "I promise there is nothing to be scared of. Trust me." Sam put a hand to the back of Wyatt's neck and gently rubbed his thumb through the hair at his nape. He pressed a kiss to the top of Wyatt's head. "I promise," Sam repeated, kissing his head again for good measure. Wyatt squeezed, holding Sam almost painfully tightly for a few seconds, in what Sam hoped was acknowledgment and acceptance of Sam's words. "Will you let me prove it to you?" Sam asked.

He felt Wyatt nod.

"Good," Sam said, running a hand over the back of Wyatt's head, smoothing his hair down. "Thank you."

Their moment was interrupted by the sound of boots moving swiftly over gravel. Sam had completely forgotten that Dan was lurking a few yards away like the world's most annoyingly dutiful bodyguard. Wyatt and Sam pulled back from one another to look in the direction of the noise. In the dim amount of light that emanated from the lodge to their place in the yard, Sam could just make out the bulky shape of Dan briskly sneaking along the tree line path. Against everything Dan had ever taught Sam, he wanted to follow him to see what had his hackles up. "Come on," Sam whispered to Wyatt, grabbing his hand and pulling him toward where Dan was slinking in the shadows.

"Is that a good idea?" Wyatt asked, allowing Sam to drag him forward.

"Probably not," Sam said, his voice full of mischief.

"For the love of Euclid," Wyatt muttered, following along reluctantly.

Sam grinned to himself as he narrowed the distance between them and Dan. Wyatt was so cute when he was being a goody-goody math nerd.

It was actually a real testament to how well Dan had done his job that Sam felt confident enough to goof around and follow him. Sam rarely ever thought back to the incident that had caused him to agree to hire Dan in the first place. He had been meeting Mara for lunch at a restaurant in LA, and a group of fans had stopped him on the sidewalk. He'd stopped to take selfies and say hello to them, but when he'd told them he had to go, one of them grabbed his arm, holding it too tight, her eyes a little too wild. She'd told him that he should at least pay her a little more attention, given how much she loved him. She'd pulled her shirt sleeve up to show him the *Ominous*-themed tattoo on her forearm. There were numbers beneath it, and Sam's blood had chilled when he'd realized it was his birthday. Not his character's birthday. His actual birthday. When he'd tried to pull away from her again, she clutched at him, her fingernails leaving marks in his skin. Thankfully, her friends had been embarrassed and pulled her off him. But that encounter had shown Sam that fans could become obsessive, and when Matt and Clark had seen the fingernail marks on his arm, they'd insisted he hire someone to accompany him when he was in public. And that's how he'd ended up with the best HO in town, Danson. And since then, Sam had always felt safe.

A few yards in front of them, Dan had stopped in his tracks, like he was waiting in ambush. When they got close enough to see his face, Sam could tell that Dan was looking right at them, and he was not happy to see them.

"What's the word, Dan-o?" Sam whispered, like they were on a stakeout.

"Get back to the house," Dan hissed.

Ice hit Sam's belly. Dan didn't look like he was kidding. *Shit.* Was there actually someone out there? He immediately looked to Wyatt, whose eyes were wide. What an idiot Sam was dragging him out after whatever threat Dan suspected. The sick feeling Sam had had in his gut when that girl had dug her claws into him returned, the worst kind of déjà vu. No way did he want Wyatt near any situation like that. Ever.

A branch snapped in the trees to their left. Dan's head whirled toward the noise, and Sam and Wyatt exchanged a panicked look. Sam squeezed Wyatt's hand, about to pull him back toward the house, when they heard something else. Was that...?

"Jesus." Dan said it like a curse, dropping his head like he felt such a potent mix of relief and annoyance that he couldn't hold his head up properly.

"What?" Sam whisper-hissed.

Another branch cracked; this time followed by the unmistakable sound of giggles. And then a woman shushing the giggler, which lead to more giggles on the part of the original giggler and the shusher.

"Get out here," Dan hollered into the trees. "Now."

Frantic whispers could be heard followed by the sound of shuffling jacket-clad bodies out of the woods. Dan stood with his hands on his hips, waiting for the offenders to emerge from the woods, Sam and Wyatt still hand in hand behind him.

And out tripped Mara, followed by a slightly unsteady Harlow. And, rounding out the trio, Tyson stepped out of the trees last, smoothing his stocking cap down and acting so nonchalant it was humorous.

At the sight of his sister's throuple stumbling out of the woods like teenagers caught at a bonfire party with wine coolers in their possession, Sam couldn't help but bark out a laugh. When Sam looked at Wyatt, he was holding his lips tight, giving it his damnedest not to break down into giggles as well.

"What the hell's the matter with you three?" Dan was

pissed off. And a pissed-off Dan was enough to chastise even Mara.

"We just needed some privacy," Mara explained. "The lodge is so crowded, and Clark said he'd listen for Milo, and we..." When she looked at Harlow and then Tyson, who were all doing their best to look contrite, they all broke into guilty giggles.

"Oh, my mistake," Dan said, his voice dripping in sarcasm. "Who cares about the safety and security of everyone in this lodge. What's that compared to the need to make out with your...people...in private."

At that, Mara, Harlow, and Tyson's faces did sober. "We're sorry, Dan," Harlow said. "We weren't thinking. Of course you're trying to do your job and don't need us undermining that."

Dan grunted something that seemed to be gruff acceptance of her apology.

"Just get your asses in the house," Dan said. The three of them nodded and dutifully marched toward the lodge.

Sam and Wyatt were about to follow them when Dan barked at them next. "And that goes for you two as well. No more grab ass in the yard. Get inside and stay inside." Then he placed a hand on Sam's shoulder to shunt him forward. "Now."

"Yes, sir," Sam said, doing his very best not to look at Wyatt out of the corner of his eye as they went back to the lodge. He was pretty sure he heard Dan muttering something about deserving a raise.

# Chapter Fourteen

## Wyatt

W yatt had never seen anything quite like Jasper and Matt's wedding ceremony. At the top of the mountain, snow-capped peaks and pale blue sky as their backdrop, the grooms stood in front of a wooden arch draped in greenery and full-bloomed white flowers. Jasper was stunning and sophisticated as always in a classic black tuxedo. His pocket square was a slate blue color that matched the suit Matt wore. Matt was an absolute knockout in his custom slim-fit suit, the steely blue color complementing his pale skin and making his platinum hair pop. His tattoos peeked out of his cuffs and collar, adding a bit more edge to the formal look. Delicate gold hoops glinted in his brow and lip, and in his ears were shiny black plugs. The men faced one another, their hands clasped between them, and even from where Wyatt sat in the second row of the assembled crowd, he could see the love radiating in the teary smiles they shared. Wyatt had never actually attended a wedding before, and he was taken aback by the wave of emotion he felt as he listened to the men express their devotion to one another, making promises of lifelong partnership.

Much to Wyatt's relief, Uncle Bo did an excellent job of officiating, not bringing in any of the showmanship Wyatt had feared he'd use to upstage the grooms. As Bowen spoke the official words of the ceremony—the "I, Jasper" and "I, Matt" stuff—and the grooms dutifully repeated their lines, Wyatt's gaze drifted away from the grooms. On Jasper's side, his business partner and best friend, Gwen, held the position of "best woman." Next to her were Grayson and Finn, and Wyatt mentally noted how surreal his life was that he was attending a wedding where two of the biggest celebrities in the world were just casually groomsmen. On Matt's side, directly beside him was his best friend, Ethan. Next to him was Clark, then Mara, and finally, Sam. During the rehearsal, Wyatt had questioned if it weren't odd for Matt to have one more attendant than Jasper, to which everyone had told him to forget about what was traditional, to which Wyatt had agreed. He should have known better than to expect anything "normal" of this wedding. And it was so much the lovelier for that, he thought, as he eyed Sam.

Sam looked fantastic in his suit. He was a slight man, but he didn't look delicate. More...mischievous, somehow. Like he was about to jump up and click his heels or start break dancing at any moment. His red hair was combed back from his forehead, and it fluttered slightly in the breeze. Wyatt knew it wouldn't last until dinner in the careful style. It would be a messy mass of tufts before the ceremony was through. Sam was never one to stay prim and proper long. It didn't suit him. He was perpetually boyish and lively, and that was part of what Wyatt loved so much about him.

Wyatt carefully took in all the details of Sam's appearance, wanting to commit all of them to memory. From his shiny caramel-colored shoes to the long lines of his legs in the gray suit pants, and the way the buttoned jacket showed off his narrow waist. He was wearing one of the more-lopsided boutonnieres from the bunch, but he stood tall and proud, clearly honored to be supporting his brother on this special day. He was beautiful. So beautiful Wyatt's chest hurt. And when Sam's eyes flicked into the crowd, finding Wyatt's, and Sam's lips curved up at the ends, Wyatt felt light-headed from the rush of it. He held his gaze, and for the first time since he'd known Sam, Wyatt left them wide open, revealing every emotion he felt for him. If he wasn't mistaken, he could feel the same intensity reflected back at him from Sam. It was potent. And terrifying.

When the crowd around Wyatt stood and cheered, hoots and hollers and applause ringing out across the mountaintop, Wyatt finally broke eye contact with Sam to witness the grooms' epic first kiss as husbands. He clapped along with everyone else, and he couldn't help himself from the secret wish that that could be him and Sam one day. He quickly buried that one back in the lockbox deep down in the most foolish depth of his heart, where it belonged.

The reception was just as magnificent as the ceremony. The vaulted-ceilinged rooms of the reception hall had windows that rose into the sky, showing off the setting sun behind the mountain at dusk. There were thousands of candles on white-linen tables with rustic centerpieces of greenery and the same white blooms from the ceremony arch. A magazine-worthy wedding cake had its own table in one corner, and beside it was a table filled with bubbling champagne flutes. At one end of the space, there was a dance floor, and a DJ was setting up at a table against the far wall. Jasper and Matt were moving hand in hand through the crowd, greeting everyone with hugs and the widest grins Wyatt had ever seen on either of their faces.

The crowd wasn't particularly large, both because it was a destination wedding and because of the security and privacy factors, but Wyatt estimated a good fifty guests in attendance all told, if he included the bodyguards. Speaking of bodyguards, Wyatt caught a glimpse of Sam and Danson chatting by a window across the room. Dan was scowling, and Sam seemed to be yammering on enthusiastically about something, which Wyatt had come to recognize as business as usual for the two of them. Wyatt was grateful that Sam had such a dependable personal security guard. He'd heard through the grapevine about the scare Sam had had with the fan that had led to his hiring Danson. Wyatt had never wanted to gouge someone's eyes out as viciously as he had the fan that had hurt and scared Sam. But he felt that Sam was in good hands with Danson, and Wyatt was exceedingly thankful for that. Wyatt didn't even want to think about all the ways in which Danson might be necessary to Sam's safety, so he shook the thought off and went for the table of champagne.

As Wyatt reached for a glass, he was intercepted by his uncle. "Well, I killed that," Bowen said, raising his fist for a bump.

Wyatt bumped his fist in return before grabbing his champagne and taking a sip. "You know, Uncle Bo, I think that's what most guests will say about the ceremony. 'That officiant really nailed it.'" He smirked at his uncle, who grabbed two champagne flutes from the table and followed Wyatt into the seating area.

"I did nail it," Bowen said, and Wyatt wasn't sure if he

hadn't caught the sarcasm or had simply chosen to ignore it. Either was equally possible with Bowen.

They reached a table where Clark and the Mara throuple sat. Bowen handed one of the champagne flutes to Clark, who took it with what almost looked like a smile. Clark was a bristly fellow, but his grumpiness slipped sometimes with Bowen, and that was what Wyatt appreciated most about Clark. He let Bowen in. He could only hope some of that was rubbing off on Sam. He knew Sam looked up to Clark. Maybe some of Clark's influence had made an impression on him. One thing Wyatt continuously wondered over the last several days was what accounted for Sam's change of heart when it came to him. With the wedding and everything, he hadn't really dared dig too deeply into that. But as the weekend was rapidly passing by, the thought was more persistent. *Why?* That was what Wyatt really needed to know. Why had Sam changed his mind about him? And would he change it back?

Wyatt didn't have too much time to get in his head about that, however, because just then servers came out with salad plates, and everyone took their seats to enjoy dinner. There was a salad course and a main course (of which Wyatt had opted for the fish). For dessert, the magnificent wedding cake was cut by the grooms in the manner necessary for the photographer and videographer to get loving shots of the two of them slicing into the cake and feeding one another, and then the servers brought slices around for everyone, pouring coffee and dropping off new bottles of champagne at each table. Wyatt's table was fairly quiet while they ate the exquisite raspberry-filled vanilla cake, everyone sipping coffees or swigging champagne jovially. At least it was quiet for a table that included three Deerwood siblings. There was cheerful chatter and good-natured laughter as Mara, Harlow, and Tyson conversed and took turns holding Milo, who was stuffing his chubby cheeks with frosting. Clark and Bowen whispered to each other, and Wyatt had a pretty good suspicion he didn't want to know anything his uncle was saying into his husband's ear right then.

That left Sam and Wyatt, who looked up from their cake and smiled at one another every so often but didn't speak much. It wasn't an uncomfortable silence; it was more of a charged silence. Like there was anticipation brewing between them, but for what, exactly, Wyatt didn't know. He was too afraid to hope. The night before, after they'd been sent back into the lodge by Danson, he and Sam had gotten ready for bed and climbed in together. They'd slid close, and by some unspoken agreement, they'd both known what to do. Or that's how Wyatt saw it. They'd kissed softly, and Sam had brushed back the hair from Wyatt's forehead. Then Sam had kissed his forehead, and said, "roll over." Wyatt had, facing away from Sam, and Sam had curved around him, tugging him in tight, Wyatt's back to Sam's chest. Sam had then kissed the back of Wyatt's shoulder once and whispered, "Sleep." And Wyatt had. And it had been perfect.

But Wyatt being who he was, and this...whatever it was happening with Sam being something potentially life-changing for him, he couldn't help analyzing every word and interaction he'd had with Sam since they'd arrived in Vail. What did it mean? And how could he hold on to it? To Sam? Was that even an option? It felt much too fragile to bring up any of these major questions with Sam. The last thing he wanted was to push Sam away now that he finally had him. But Wyatt mentally scolded himself for that thought. He didn't "have" Sam. And thinking that he did would only lead to more heartbreak.

Wyatt was vaguely aware of the tinkling of glasses and people standing up at the microphone to give their speeches to the grooms. Jasper's best woman, Gwen, must have been hilarious because the crowd was barking out laughs as she spoke, though Wyatt couldn't focus on what she was saying. At the end of her speech, she was teary-eyed, and Jasper stood to hug her tightly. The crowd "aww"ed. Then the mic went to Ethan, Matt's best man. Ethan was a cute, gangly guy with dark curls and glasses, and he was clearly very uneasy speaking to a crowd. His husband, a super-hot man with broad shoulders threatening the seams of his suit coat, stood up with him for moral support, and it was one of the sweetest things Wyatt had seen. Ethan's speech was short and heartfelt, and Matt stood to hug him when it was done, squeezing Ethan tightly. Ethan patted Matt on the back a bit awkwardly, but they shared a sincere smile, and all of them sat down again. Jasper and Matt stood then, taking the mic to thank everyone for traveling to Vail to celebrate with them. They encouraged everyone to drink plenty, and they threatened the crowd that they better be out on the dance floor "or else." Everyone applauded and went back to their cake and drinks while the DJ finished setting up for the dance portion of the evening.

Beside Wyatt, Sam shed his coat and his tie, undoing two buttons at his collar. People in the crowd were milling around now, some of them using the restroom or wandering to the exits to smoke or make phone calls. In the chaos, Sam slid his chair closer to Wyatt's to be heard when he spoke to him. "Do you think that Wilkinson is secretly in love with Danny Boy?"

"What?" Wyatt followed Sam's gaze to the room's

perimeter where Danson, Wilkinson, and Hicks were stationed. They'd been wandering around the edges of the room all evening, sometimes slipping outside for a few minutes, but at that moment the three of them stood side by side, Danson in the middle. "Why on earth would you think that?" Wyatt shook his head at Sam in fond exasperation.

"Look how he's standing," Sam said, nodding his head in their direction. "He's way closer to Dan-o than necessary."

Wyatt didn't see that one bit. He was a perfectly respectable distance from Dan. "I don't think..."

"Look!" Sam's eyes widened and sparkled, and he'd slapped a hand on Wyatt's knee for emphasis. "He was just staring at Dan, and then when Dan looked over at him, he averted his eyes." Sam nodded vigorously. "I'm telling you; he wants in Dan's pants."

Wyatt rolled his eyes at Sam. "You're insane."

Sam grinned back at him. "Wanna bet?"

"You want to place a wager on whether or not Wilkinson wants to sleep with Danson?"

"Yes," Sam said.

"No," Wyatt said.

"Why not? Cuz you know I'm right?" Sam raised a brow.

"No," Wyatt said again. "Because we're not betting on the sex lives of your personal security officers."

Sam pouted. "Please?"

Wyatt shook his head. He was clearly never going to win this one. "Fine," he relented. "If Wilkinson confesses his burning desire to get Danson in the sack, you win."

Sam perked up again. "What do I get when I win?"

Wyatt ran his hands over his face to gather his patience. Not that he was actually in any way impatient with Sam. In fact, he loved every second of interactions like this. "What do you want if you win?"

Sam gave him a sly smile that was borderline dirty, and the hand he'd placed on Wyatt's knee earlier, which he hadn't removed, slid a few inches higher then squeezed. "An IOU," he said. And the sexy way he said that, combined with the teasing squeeze of his fingers on Wyatt's thigh would have had Wyatt agreeing to perform karaoke in his underwear in front of this entire crowd.

"Deal," Wyatt managed, his voice sounding much throatier than he'd expected.

Sam licked his lips and stared into Wyatt's eyes in a way that had Wyatt's neck flushing and caused him to shift in his seat. "It's on," Sam said. And then he winked. Wyatt let out an unsteady laugh and Sam's hand inched a bit higher on his thigh.

"Attention, people!" The loud voice coming from the speakers jolted Wyatt back to the reception, he and Sam both jumping slightly and turning toward the DJ who was speaking into the mic over by the dance floor. "We're about to get his party started!" The crowd cheered and applauded. "We're going to begin with the grooms' first dance. After that, get up and join us on the dance floor!" He set the mic down and started to play "Adore You" by Harry Styles. The grooms went out onto the floor and danced in a way that Wyatt hadn't known either of them could, and the crowd let out whoops and hollers. Sam and Wyatt stood and made their way to the edge of the dance floor to get a better look.

"Do you think Matty actually took dance lessons?" Sam's eyes were on his brother, where he was twirled around by Jasper, a wide grin on his face.

"It would appear so," Wyatt said, equally mesmerized by the men moving smoothly to the beat of the music.

"That's so sweet," Sam said. "Who knew Matty was a romantic at heart?"

Wyatt looked at Sam from the corner of his eye. He looked so beautiful in the dim light from the strands of bulbs hanging over the dance floor. A look of amazement and pure joy for his brother shone through him.

"People surprise you sometimes," Wyatt said.

Sam smiled and reached out for Wyatt's hand, though he kept his eyes on his brother and his new husband twirling around the dance floor. Wyatt took his hand and laced their fingers together, holding tight.

# Chapter Fifteen

## Sam

The last half hour of the reception, all Sam could think about was getting Wyatt back to the lodge. He couldn't stop thinking about how good it had felt to hold him in his arms the night before. There was a deep feeling of rightness as he'd felt the rise and fall of Wyatt's body against his own chest. He'd lost track of how many kisses he'd placed on the back of Wyatt's head during the night. He had been well aware that he'd never before held anything so precious, and he hadn't taken that for granted. He just hoped that he'd get to do it again later that night.

Earlier in the evening, they'd danced together once, and it had been lovely, but they really didn't want to cause any speculation about whatever was happening between them, so they'd not gotten too cozy with one another. They'd spent the evening drinking and dancing, Wyatt actually taking a turn around the floor with his uncle and then Clark, then finding a seat near the dance floor to watch the rest of the revelers. Sam, in true life-of-the-party fashion, had found himself in the center of a dance circle more than once, busting out his best moves. He'd had a dance-off with Harlow, who was, admittedly, even better than he was with rhythm and showmanship. More than once, Sam had caught Wyatt looking at him a little...hungrily. And Sam had absolutely loved it. He'd taken the opportunity to sway his hips just a bit more seductively, even shooting Wyatt a wink here and there, which had caused Wyatt to blush and avert his eyes. It was so cute Sam could hardly stand it.

The crowd had dwindled down to mainly just the people who were staying at the lodge, with the additions of Gwen and her husband, Ethan and his husband, and a couple of others that Sam didn't recognize. The DJ had started to slowly work the energy back down from Nicki Minaj to Van Morrison in a gradual progression. While "Into the Mystic" swelled over the space, Sam looked to Wyatt's seat, seeing it vacant. He wondered where Wyatt had wandered off to, hoping he hadn't gone back to the lodge without him. A tap on Sam's shoulder had him whirling around, and there was Wyatt. "I was wondering," Wyatt said, glancing around the dance floor conspicuously before stepping into Sam's space, "if I could have one more dance before we go back."

Sam loved the sound of "we" in that sentence, and he agreed, placing his hands on Wyatt's waist and pulling him in a bit closer than they'd dared the first time they'd danced. At this point in the night, Sam reasoned, everyone was either too drunk or too distracted by their own dance partners to pay much attention to them. Wyatt's hands landed on his shoulders, but they quickly slid up to the back of Sam's neck, the warm pads of Wyatt's fingers sending tingles across Sam's skin. Wyatt's slim waist felt good under Sam's hands, and he was dying to sneak his fingers under Wyatt's shirt to get a feel of his bare skin, but he didn't dare.

Almost like Wyatt could read Sam's mind, he smirked at Sam. "Soon," he whispered, moving in a bit closer until their bodies grazed one another as they moved. The anticipation that one whispered word elicited in Sam was nearly too much. He swallowed hard and tried his best not to blatantly grind himself against Wyatt's leg. He repeated Wyatt's promise in his own mind: soon.

A haziness hung over them, a combination of the white lights twinkling overhead, the crooning voice of Van Morrison on the speakers, and the dizzying feeling of undeniable connection between them. Sam had no idea how he'd ever been able to deny it the first time Wyatt had told him how he felt. He'd been lying to himself, that was for sure. He'd had himself convinced that while he loved Wyatt, of course, it was as his best friend. Now, he knew that to be true, but that it was also more than that. And, if he was truly honest with himself then, he would have to admit that he'd been afraid. He'd been so terrified that any change to their relationship could cause Wyatt to leave. And that would never be something he'd be okay with. And it had backfired. Denying how he really felt had pushed Wyatt away, and if what had been happening between them over the last week was actually real, Sam would never let it go again. But how should he proceed now? What could he do to ensure he didn't ruin everything again? He didn't know. He supposed he would let Wyatt take the lead.

Speaking of which, the song ended, but neither of them let go immediately. "Sam?" Wyatt said, his voice a bit shaky.

"Wyatt," Sam said, smiling at him.

"Let's go back to the lodge."

Wyatt didn't have to ask him twice.

Dan had been particularly annoying on the ride back to the lodge. He'd kept chatting away about their departure plans—packing and what time they needed to leave the lodge to get to the airport. It was a major downer thinking about leaving Vail and returning to LA. It wasn't that Sam didn't want to get back home and back to work; he absolutely did. But he wasn't ready for that to happen just yet. He wanted to have this one more night with Wyatt before having to think about tomorrow or what was next. Wyatt was especially quiet in the back seat of the car beside Sam, and Sam was dying to know what he was thinking. But he was also too afraid to ask.

When Dan parked in front of the lodge, he'd gruffly said, "Wait here," and climbed out to do his check before letting Sam go inside. Wyatt kept up with his silent routine, and Sam's nerves were starting to bubble up, threatening to boil over, but he really didn't want to say something stupid or push Wyatt right then. So, he simply took Wyatt's hand in his and held it, looking out into the blackness out his window until Dan returned. Dan appeared in the porch light, gesturing it was all clear. Once inside, Wyatt and Sam both beelined to their room, Sam muttering a goodnight to Dan and promising to set his alarm.

Sam followed Wyatt inside their room, closing their door softly behind him once they were inside. Wyatt didn't give Sam time to so much as speak before he was on him. They hadn't even turned on the light, and Wyatt's hands were on Sam's chest, backing him into the closed door. Wyatt's mouth found Sam's in the dark, a rough pressure Sam hadn't felt from Wyatt before. Wyatt groaned and pushed his body into Sam's. Sam could feel the firm oak of the door behind his back and the firm pressure of Wyatt's hips pressing into his own. Wyatt's hands slid up his chest before his fingers dug into Sam's shoulders. Wyatt ground against him, sparks shooting through Sam's entire body as their erections rubbed together through their clothing. Sam quickly tugged at the fabric of Wyatt's shirt, pulling it free from his pants so he could slip his hands beneath it and finally feel the delicious, smooth skin of Wyatt's back. Wyatt's mouth opened on a gasp as Sam rocked his hips into Wyatt's. Sam smiled with smugness at the way Wyatt responded to every single touch and movement he made, like everything about him turned Wyatt on. That was incredibly flattering. And sexy.

Sam took the opportunity to get his lips on the skin of Wyatt's throat, which tasted salty and hot. He darted his tongue out to take a proper taste of the flesh there, and Wyatt's hips jerked. Sam chuckled into Wyatt's neck, inhaling the scent of him. It was a familiar smell, though not necessarily one he associated with Wyatt. He paused, taking a deeper inhale.

Wyatt pulled back, placing his hands on Sam's face and turning it to look at him. "What's wrong?" Even in the dark room, Sam could see the concern in Wyatt's furrowed brow.

"Are you wearing my cologne?" Sam raised a brow he wasn't sure Wyatt could see, but he knew Wyatt would pick up on the teasing in his tone. Sam remembered seeing the cologne bottle in the bathroom, and now his suspicions were about to be confirmed: Wyatt was wearing the same cologne Sam wore.

"What?" Wyatt averted his eyes and tried to bury his face in Sam's neck. Sam let him get one open-mouthed kiss in, which felt like heaven, but he would not be deterred. He pushed Wyatt back and demanded an answer.

"Did you wear my cologne?" Sam repeated. "Tell me the truth, Wyatt Price, or I will not kiss you any more tonight."

Wyatt scoffed. "I don't believe you."

"Try me," Sam said, fighting a giggle.

"If you must know," Wyatt said, taking a step back and shedding his jacket, "I most certainly am not wearing your cologne."

Sam's eyes followed Wyatt's long fingers as they opened the buttons of his shirt deftly. Sam really wanted to help him, but he was also well aware Wyatt was trying to distract him from his line of questioning.

"Then why do you smell like me?"

"I'm not wearing your cologne," Wyatt insisted.

"Fine," Sam said. "What cologne are you wearing?"

"Mine," Wyatt said.

Sam folded his arms, trying very hard to keep his distance as Wyatt discarded his shirt to the floor and moved on to his belt. "What's it called then?"

Wyatt pulled his belt from the loops of his pants and let it fall to the floor. His fingers were on the clasp of his fly, and he looked at Sam without answering.

"What's the cologne you're wearing called, Wyatt?" Sam tried to sound stern, but he wasn't pulling it off. It was becoming increasingly clear to both of them that trying to be stern and hold out on touching Wyatt was not Sam's strong suit.

Wyatt reached one hand into his pants, sliding it into his boxers. He tilted his head back and moaned as he palmed himself.

"Damn it, Wyatt," Sam cursed. "Just tell me so I can suck you off already."

Wyatt chuckled at that, pulling his hand free from his pants.

"It's Moorside Elixir, okay," Wyatt said with a laugh. "You caught me."

"So you did wear my cologne," Sam said, triumph in his

voice. "You sneaky little liar." He moved over to Wyatt, sliding his zipper down for him and pushing his pants down, happy he could touch him again.

"I didn't," Wyatt said softly before kissing Sam's lips carefully. "I bought some," he continued, explaining himself between brief kisses. "I missed you."

Sam cupped Wyatt's face. "You bought my cologne because you missed me?"

Wyatt tried to look down, but Sam held his face in his hands, waiting for Wyatt to meet his eyes.

"Yes," Wyatt said. "I needed to feel close to you some-how...," he said, trailing off.

"Wyatt," Sam said, his voice full of emotion he couldn't even fully comprehend. "That's..."

"Embarrassing," Wyatt said, again trying to turn away. Sam held his face firmly.

"No," Sam said decisively. "It's sweet. And it makes me feel better," Sam went on, "because then I don't have to feel like I was the only one..."

"You weren't," Wyatt said.

And then they were kissing again, deep, long strokes of their tongues, brushing pressure of lips, hands groping eagerly. Sam's heart pounded hard in his chest, and his legs wobbled. Kissing had never felt like this before with anyone else. He was starting to learn, though, that everything was different with Wyatt. Wyatt's hands went to the buttons of Sam's shirt, and Sam slid his hands all over the soft skin of Wyatt's exposed stomach and chest as Wyatt stripped him. Wyatt trailed his hands down Sam's shoulders and biceps, gripping them firmly as he kissed Sam harder, walking him backward toward the bed. Wyatt shoved Sam and Sam landed on the edge of the bed, Wyatt stepping close but not following him all the way. "You should take off your pants," Wyatt said, standing there, waiting for Sam to comply.

"Yes, sir," Sam said, quickly undoing his belt and fly, slipping out of his pants and socks. He sat back down on the bed in his boxers, eyeing Wyatt, who was likewise stripped to his underwear, looking gorgeous in the sliver of moonlight slipping past the blinds. Sam was loving this plan of letting Wyatt take the lead. Wyatt had excellent ideas.

"I think we should have sex," Wyatt said, still not touching Sam, which Sam found incredibly frustrating. And then his brain registered the words Wyatt had just spoken.

"Wait. What?"

"I want to have sex," Wyatt said. "With you. If you do, that is." Wyatt ran his hands through his hair, which he'd let hang loose, though it had been combed back neatly before they'd started mauling one another.

"I do," Sam said eagerly, nodding. "Very much so."

Wyatt nodded, as if to say, "That settles that," and then he approached Sam, slower this time, more tentatively. When he leaned over Sam, Sam could see a set to Wyatt's jaw. It was his determined face, Sam thought. Sam reached up and tugged Wyatt to him, kissing him thoroughly, but gently. Wyatt seemed to relax into the kiss, and Sam wiggled back so he was fully on the bed. Wyatt followed, straddling him on hands and knees, kissing him with increasing fervor.

"Wyatt," Sam said, as Wyatt's mouth slid down his neck and landed on his collarbone, the sharp suction pinching Sam hard enough that he jerked beneath Wyatt from the sting.

"Mmm," Wyatt said, not letting up.

"We don't have to," Sam said. He didn't want Wyatt to

be doing this to prove something or because it was their last night in Vail, or because he thought it's what Sam expected.

Wyatt pressed a kiss to his chest, then the spot he'd sucked on Sam's collarbone, then his lips. Then he looked down at Sam, so much want and affection radiating from him, it made Sam's eyes sting. "I want to," Wyatt said.

"Me too," Sam said. And he clasped the back of Wyatt's neck and pulled him down to him again.

# Chapter Sixteen

## Wyatt

Wyatt's hands were shaky as he ran them up Sam's torso. The sight of Sam beneath him, trapped beneath Wyatt's spread thighs, had Wyatt incredibly turned on. Sam's red hair was a mess, and his lips were swollen from Wyatt's rough kisses. More than how much he physically ached for Sam, Wyatt knew the pressure in his chest, the flutter in his stomach, and the unsteady breaths he expelled were due to how much he loved him. How unbelievably good it felt to be close to him like this. To connect with him in this way—a way Wyatt had only ever dreamed of.

"Look at you," Sam said, running his hands up Wyatt's bare thighs. "You're beautiful, Wyatt." Sam's eyes were locked on Wyatt's, his only movement his palms sliding over Wyatt's muscled legs. He was clearly waiting for Wyatt, wanting to go at Wyatt's pace. Wyatt lifted up on his knees and tugged his boxers off. Sam's gaze dropped to Wyatt's hard cock where it bobbed between his thighs. Sam licked his lips, but he didn't make a move. Wyatt straddled Sam again, the only thing between them the layer of cotton of Sam's boxers.

Wyatt needed to move slowly. He was overwhelmed by everything he was feeling, both Sam's body beneath his and the thumping of his heart in his chest, the chemicals coursing through his veins telling him that this was what getting your deepest desire felt like. And there was nothing that could have prepared him for it. He leaned down, bracing himself on wobbly arms, and pressed his lips to Sam's tentatively. Somehow, being naked made him bashful, his vulnerability on full display. Sam's hands went to Wyatt's sides, caressing him as he opened his mouth, his tongue sliding forward shyly, just brushing Wyatt's. Wyatt's cock slid against Sam's stomach, and he was certain the tip was leaking onto Sam's skin. The thought made him shiver, his desire deepening even further. The friction on his dick as Sam started to rock his hips up into Wyatt had Wyatt amping up the kiss, and Sam's hands slid to the swell of Wyatt's firm ass pulling him even closer. Wyatt's weight was resting on Sam more fully, and Sam seemed to love it, wriggling beneath him desperately, a needy moan escaping as he dug his fingers into Wyatt's ass cheeks, taking proper handfuls.

Wyatt was the one moaning then, pulling his mouth from Sam's and maneuvering down the bed far enough to get his fingers into Sam's waistband. He glanced at Sam for permission, and Sam nodded, his eyes wild with wanting. Wyatt pulled Sam's boxers off, exposing his hard cock, which stood at full attention, the head resting up against Sam's stomach. Wyatt admired it for a quick moment before crawling back up, kissing Sam hard and fast on the mouth, then getting up off the bed. "I'll be right back," he told Sam over his shoulder as he disappeared into the bathroom. He came back a moment later with a bottle of lube. His cheeks were flushed, and he knew he looked crazed and desperate. Sam watched him come back to the bed, a lazy smile on his face. Wyatt had never seen anything so sexy—Sam's impish, freckled smile paired with his smoking hot, naked body stretched out and waiting—Wyatt was already leaking for him.

Wyatt suddenly felt self-conscious. He realized that he and Sam had never discussed who would be doing what, exactly. Wyatt assumed that Sam was a top, or at least vers. He also assumed Sam knew he was a bottom. But maybe that wasn't obvious? He certainly didn't want to do something embarrassing like ask Sam to fuck him, if Sam was expecting to be the one getting fucked. Sam must have registered Wyatt's inner turmoil, because he slid up, leaning back against the headboard. "Hey," Sam said, his tone soft and careful. "What's wrong?"

"Oh," Wyatt said, perching on the end of the bed facing Sam. He absently passed the lube bottle from one hand to the other. "I was just wondering..." Wyatt felt his cheeks positively flame with embarrassment. Sam looked at him with concern, tilting his head to the side.

"Wondering...?"

"You know," Wyatt said. "How to...proceed?"

Sam's brows were still pulled together in confusion, and he ran a hand through his messy red locks. "Proceed?"

"Yeah," Wyatt said. "Like..." He held up the lube bottle. "I wanted to..." He nodded to Sam's cock, which was still straining upward, thankfully, despite Wyatt's awkward intermission to the main event.

Sam's eyes widened. "You wanted to lube me up?"

Wyatt swallowed. "Yeah, your..." He nodded again, and Sam's lips twitched. He fisted his cock and stroked it slowly.

"My dick," Sam said. "Yes, you can lube up my dick." His smile spread, and Wyatt's dick hardened further at Sam's confirmation that he wanted to fuck Wyatt. And since that was settled, Wyatt got to work, popping open the lube and pouring it into his palm. He wrapped his palm around Sam's shaft, and Sam groaned loudly, his head tilting back against the headboard. Wyatt climbed back on top of him, straddling his thighs as he thoroughly lubed Sam's long cock. Wyatt leaned in to kiss Sam, his hand still working him, until Sam pulled Wyatt's hand away. "Getting too close," Sam said, reaching for the lube. He drizzled it all over the fingers of his right hand, and Wyatt rose up on his knees, kissing Sam furiously as Sam's fingers slid down the crease of his ass. While Sam took his time opening Wyatt up at a tortuously teasing pace, Wyatt was reveling in the feel of Sam's slick cock sliding against his as they made out. Nothing had ever felt as good as this moment, the anticipation tingling low in his belly as Sam pulled out the two fingers that had been pumping into him. Sam grabbed the lube and added a bit more to his dick before urging Wyatt on. "Guide me in," he said, his voice raspy and lust drunk.

Wyatt firmly gripped the base of Sam's cock, got up on his knees, and positioned Sam at his hole. Sam's hands had gone back to the slow strokes up and down Wyatt's thighs, and Wyatt took a breath in and released it as he slowly worked himself down onto Sam's cock. They both groaned as Sam's dick filled him up, and Wyatt closed his eyes and focused on his breathing for a few moments, working past the sting.

Once he'd adjusted to the fullness, Wyatt opened his eyes to find Sam staring up at him. Sweat dampened Sam's hair, and he had a determined look on his face, his brows pulled together as if in concentration.

Wyatt slowly lifted up, and Sam dug his fingers into Wyatt's hips, snapping his eyes shut again. "Wyatt. Jesus." Sam bit out the words as Wyatt rose up a bit further on Sam's cock before sliding back down. Their shared groans were loud, and Wyatt would have been self-conscious about that, fearing that Danson or someone else might be able to hear them, but he was too consumed with the delicious pressure of Sam inside him to care. Wyatt continued to move up and down, rhythmically as best he could. He was no sex expert. He'd mostly only had sex with Bernard, his trusty blue dildo. And now it was Sam thrusting inside him. Whether it was the rogue thought of Bernard, the amazing shock of pleasure zipping through him as Sam thrust deep, or the overwhelming emotion he felt when Sam met his eyes and smiled, Wyatt wasn't sure, but he felt the insane urge to laugh and cry at the same time. Like his heart and his brain were short-circuiting trying to comprehend the reality of what was happening. But one thing he was sure of was that he didn't want to miss a second of this, so he focused his attention back on Sam. He leaned down to take Sam's mouth in a hard, slow kiss. Sam's tongue was wild and eager, and his hands gripped Wyatt's ass. Wyatt rode him all the while, feeling the pleasure brewing in his balls as his cock rubbed between their bodies.

Wyatt's lips found Sam's neck, then collarbone, pressing kisses between his mutterings of "feels so good," and the groans of Sam's name as Sam plunged in and out of him in rhythm with Wyatt's own movements.

Sam's thrusts sped up, and he splayed his hands flat against Wyatt's lower back, urging him down onto Sam's cock harder and deeper with each rock of his hips. Wyatt felt himself hurtling toward the edge when he felt Sam's lips press a feverish kiss to his head, and Sam said, "I love you. I love you so much, Wyatt."

Wyatt's entire body lit up at those words, heat and white lightning zipping through his veins. Something about hearing those words flipped a switch, and Wyatt was coming all over Sam's stomach and chest, his body pulsing and squeezing around Sam as the heat spread to his extremities. Sam wrapped his arms around Wyatt, pulling him in close as he continued to thrust into him. Wyatt collapsed into his arms, panting. He felt aftershocks as Sam continued to peg his prostate, though Wyatt had turned mostly boneless. He managed to mutter "I love you too," into Sam's chest, which was all it took to have Sam coming too, his cock pulsing deep inside Wyatt, filling him up, which Wyatt absolutely relished.

Then Sam was panting too, but he kept his arms gripped tightly around Wyatt. Wyatt felt another kiss to his head, and he smiled against Sam's freckled chest. Wyatt pressed a kiss to one of the freckles nearest him, mentally planning to kiss every single freckle on Sam's body in the near future. They were quiet, letting their hearts slow down.

Eventually, Sam whispered, "That was perfect."

Warmth spread through Wyatt's insides. He couldn't agree more. "It really was," he said. He reluctantly rolled off Sam, kissing him on the lips before flopping onto his back. They were both a sticky mess, but Wyatt knew his legs couldn't carry him if he tried, so he simply lay back and waited for Sam to get a damp washcloth to clean them up. Wyatt could not only feel some of his own release on his stomach but also Sam's release trickling out of him. It felt very dirty and very, very good. Wyatt had never let anyone come inside him before, but he was happy to have shared the experience with Sam. It did feel more intimate, and that was what making love to Sam had been—intimate. They'd crossed another line they couldn't uncross, and while that thought scared Wyatt terribly, he didn't ever want to go back. He wasn't entirely sure how they were to proceed, but at that moment, after Sam carefully cleaned him up and curled into his side, resting his head on Wyatt's chest and slinging a leg over one of Wyatt's, he didn't need to worry about it. He hadn't a single care in the world.

Wyatt pulled Sam in even closer, and he took a page from Sam's book, pressing a kiss to Sam's still-damp hair. Even in his countless fantasies about getting together with Sam, his imagination had never even come close to the reality of how incredible it felt. The joy was so intense, his ribs ached with it. The swelling of his heart threatened to burst his chest right open, splaying him wide, helpless in his love for Sam. He'd somehow always suspected that Sam Deerwood would be the death of him, one way or another. He grinned to himself at the thought, snuggling Sam in even more tightly against him.

*Bring it on, Sam.* Totally worth it.

# Chapter Seventeen

## Sam

"You will not stop to talk to anyone."

"I know, I know," Sam said, watching the city of Denver come into view from the window of their rental car.

"No autographs," Dan continued, not acknowledging Sam's response in the slightest. "Not one selfie."

"What about half a selfie? Like if someone only wants a pic of my good side," Sam said, angling his face exaggeratedly in Dan's direction.

"No," Dan said, not taking his eyes off the road as they entered the Denver city limits.

"I got it, Dan," Sam said, more seriously. "I want a repeat of the last airport experience even less than you do."

Dan huffed and nodded his head subtly, which Sam took to mean he was appeased by Sam's understanding of their airport plan of action.

"So," Dan said, and Sam perked up at his tone. He sounded like he was unsure of himself, which was not at all Dan's MO. Sam turned his attention to him, watching Dan carefully as he followed the GPS's instructions. "I think we should poach Wilkinson. We're going to want the best, not to mention I don't have the patience to work with a rookie from the agency. They're the worst. No." Dan nodded, as if something—Sam had no clue what—had just been settled. Sam noticed Dan's grip loosen a bit, his knuckles coloring back to Dan's skin tone, rather than the whitish hue they'd been moments earlier. "Hicks isn't going to like it, of course," Dan said, almost as an afterthought, as he continued to maneuver the streets of Denver.

Sam was quiet, waiting to see if Dan was finished with his unintelligible, one-sided conversation. When it seemed that he was, Sam asked the most pressing question. "What the hell you talkin' about, Dan-o?"

"Wilkinson," Dan said, as if that cleared everything right up.

Sam raised his brows at Dan, in a "You're going to need to elaborate" gesture.

Dan frowned. "Patrick Wilkinson. Personal security to Finn Everett? We just stayed in a house with the man for a week? Surely you—"

"I know who Wilkinson is," Sam said in exasperation. "Mean Keanu. We all know and love the man. What about Wilkinson? You want to pounce on him or something? Because that's something I am all in favor of, Danny Boy. You two together," Sam fanned himself. "Hot."

Dan's scowl deepened and he shook his head as he took the exit for the airport. "Not pounce. I said poach. Poach. Steal. Swipe. Nothing to do with pouncing."

"That's less fun," Sam said, his voice glum. "But I still need to buy a vowel here. You're not making a whole lotta sense, Big Dan."

"I mean we should convince Wilkinson to jump ship from Finn. We need to get him."

"For what? Am I too much for you to handle on your own?" Sam batted his lashes in Dan's direction. "Because if you want to get Wilkinson to help you...wrangle me..." Sam started fanning himself again. "Then I'm on board. Enthusiastically." He flashed Dan his grin, which Dan's death stare tried and failed to dim.

"Not for you, dumbass," Dan said, pulling up to the parking stall for the car rental return. "For Wyatt."

"You and Wilkinson want to join up to wrangle Wyatt? Because that I'll take issue with," Sam said. "That's my man. At least...I think so. I hope so?"

"My point exactly," Dan said, cutting the engine. "If you're in a relationship with Wyatt, he's going to need personal security, too."

"What?" Sam wasn't entirely sure he followed. "Why does Wyatt need personal security? When we're together, you'll be there. That should be plenty. It's not like fans will approach him when I'm not around."

Dan turned and eyed Sam, examining his features. "You know that's not true," Dan said, his voice gentler than his normal gruff tone.

Sam felt the bottom of his stomach drop out. He'd been so caught up in the excitement of being with Wyatt again—so swept up in the feelings and the intense rush of what was happening between them—that he may have overlooked a few of the practical concerns of the two of them being together beyond the shelter of the lodge and the wedding week.

Dan led Sam quickly and efficiently to the rental car desk, then through check-in and security at the airport. They'd made their way without incident—either no one recognized Sam, or he'd looked too unapproachable to bother with; he wasn't sure which. When they'd reached the VIP lounge for their airline, Sam slumped into a chair in the corner, his carry-on and Dan taking the two seats on either side of him.

"I'll talk to Hicks," Dan said, "and we'll sort it out. We'll get someone great for Wyatt. Don't worry about that."

"That's not it," Sam said. "It's that Wyatt's not going to want personal security."

"Well, I don't think he'd like being mobbed by your fans, either," Dan said.

Sam winced. His stomach had started to do this twisting thing, which caused a general ache with an occasional sharp pang when a particularly troubling thought popped up, like the one about Sam's fans mobbing Wyatt out on the street, causing him to have a panic attack that would be all Sam's fault. "No, he definitely wouldn't," Sam admitted. His mind whirred, seeking out any possible way that this wasn't going to result in the outcome he feared most: Wyatt realizing being with Sam was not worth the trouble. He asked a question he knew the answer to, somehow hoping the answer would be different than the one he knew would come. "Are you sure it's necessary? People wouldn't really go after Wyatt, would they? I'm not Tom Holland or anything."

Dan's eyes were soft, but he held Sam's stare. "Your fans are teenagers, Sam," he said. "They don't always think before they act. They are hormonal, impulsive, and unpredictable. I don't think I have to remind you..." Dan trailed off, and Sam nodded glumly, understanding. "It would only take a couple of jealous, unstable people to hurt Wyatt."

"But most of my fans aren't like that," Sam tried to argue, ignoring the memories of that girl clawing him. "They are mostly sweet kids and their mothers. You've seen them."

"Those are the ones I let near you," Dan said. "You

don't know about the deranged ones, Sam. Hicks has cyber guys that deal with all the shit posted online. I won't even tell you the things we follow up on there. And how often the alarm sounds. Wilkinson could tell you stories about Finn's so-called fans that would give you nightmares. But I don't want you to have to worry about that. And I know you don't want Wyatt to have to worry about that, either."

Sam let his head hang, his elbows resting on his knees, his hands clasped together. Then he ran both hands over his face before sitting up. Sam's jaw was tight, and his expression hard. Determined. "Okay," he said. "I'll speak with Wyatt. See if he's on board."

Dan nodded once. "Good."

Sam nodded to himself. The twisting in his gut didn't subside. If anything, it intensified, the constant, dull ache cranking up from a three to a five on the pain scale. Sam was pretty sure he wasn't going to vomit, though, so he simply sat there, plotting what on earth he could say to Wyatt that would convince him that being with Sam was worth the trouble.

* * *

As was typical of travel days, Sam was exhausted when he finally returned home to his apartment in LA. He abandoned his luggage in the entryway and collapsed onto his bed fully clothed. He wished Wyatt was beside him to snuggle up with and nap together for about three days. But when he and Wyatt had said goodbye back at the lodge, Wyatt had been the voice of reason, saying he needed to go crash at his place. He had a half-marathon to train for, after all, and he needed to get caught up on his sleep and back on his regular schedule as soon as possible. Sam had pouted, but between Wyatt's logic and Dan's insistence that they get moving, he'd begrudgingly accepted it. But, at that moment, laying in his travel-rumpled clothing on his big, empty bed, he felt lonely. Even Dan had gone home. Sam's building had 24-hour security, and Dan and the security staff were on close terms. By "close terms" he meant that Dan had scared the shit out of everyone who worked at the apartment complex by threatening that if they didn't do their jobs, he would do his, which was to ensure swift and efficient elimination of any threat to Sam. Building security had willingly complied with any of Dan's requests since then, naturally.

The memory of Dan frightening the security guards at Sam's building had Sam recalling his earlier conversation with Dan about security for Wyatt. The gut twisting resumed in full force. Part of him still thought it was completely unnecessary. Plenty of celebrities just as famous as he was, if not even more so, walked around LA with no personal security to speak of. Didn't they? Certainly not every celebrity's partner had their own bodyguard. Sam racked his brain, trying to recall whether any celebrity couples he knew had personal security assigned to their spouses or partners. Unfortunately, most celebrities he knew who were in serious relationships were in them with other famous people. So, they did tend to both have personal security. And the other people who worked on his show who had risen to fame along with Sam were happily enjoying the single life, hitting up clubs and taking full advantage of their newfound fame.

Sam sighed and ran his hands over his face, which felt slightly grimy to the touch. He really needed a shower. But that felt like a lot of work at the moment. He'd just rest for a minute more to gain his resolve. But he had to admit, the thought of a hot shower and crawling into the bedsheets freshly washed was enticing. He took in a deep breath and then exhaled loudly as he heaved himself up to sitting. He fished his phone out of the comforter where he'd dropped it when he'd originally flopped down onto the bed. He just wanted to check in with Wyatt before he got into the shower.

Sam: Make it home safe? I just got back. Wiped. Need to shower and then crash.

He waited a few minutes for Wyatt's response. When he didn't get one, he figured he was either in the shower himself or maybe out cold after all the travel. Sam was aware by now that Wyatt needed to recharge after spending so much time people-ing. Sam plugged the phone in, leaving it on his nightstand, and made his way to the bathroom.

He'd been right; the shower felt amazing. The hot water sluicing down his back felt like heaven, and he luxuriated in the scent and feel of his own body wash as he soaped up. Not that the products stocked in the lodge hadn't been of the highest quality—they certainly had—but there was just something about your own familiar things that soothed the soul after traveling. He took his time washing and conditioning his hair, relishing the feeling of shedding the travel gunk from every inch of him. He moaned as his blunt nails scratched his scalp. Scalp scratches were criminally under-rated, and he made a mental addition to his sexy wish list of having Wyatt scratch his scalp while they showered together.

When he was thoroughly rinsed, he turned the knob to cut the water, and he stepped out onto his cozy bath mat. A thick, white towel waited on the hook beside the shower for him. He ran it over his hair vigorously before toweling off his body in a cursory manner and then wrapping the towel around his waist. He stopped by his dresser to grab a pair of navy-blue boxers, abandoning the towel on the floor when he put them on. He climbed into bed, crawling between the sheets and nuzzling down, letting out a long "ahhhh" of pleasure at the feel of being clean and in his own bed in his own home. The only thing that would make it better was if Wyatt were there too.

At that thought, he wiggled over to the side of the bed so he could reach his phone off the nightstand, hoping to see a response from Wyatt waiting for him. The notification he saw when he picked up the phone shot warmth through his insides. He did have a text from Wyatt. Sam felt his face spread into a wide grin as he slid the message open.

Wyatt: Yes. I'm home.

Hm. That was...brief. Sam reread his message to Wyatt. It had been fairly clipped, too. Tired. He wouldn't read into Wyatt's short response too much. He was likely just as beat as Sam was.

Sam: Good. Hope you get some rest. Text me later.

He hit send, and he waited. No response. He reread his last text again. He really should have used a question mark at the end rather than a period. *Text me later?* At least then Wyatt would have had to reply once more in the affirmative. Sam chuckled to himself. Wyatt was one of those people who could be so literal sometimes. If Sam texted back and said, "Why didn't you respond to my last text?" Wyatt would be confused. Sam could picture Wyatt's brows furrowing adorably, and his response: "You didn't ask me a question." Sam grinned and placed his phone face down on the nightstand. That was Wyatt for you. And with that thought in his mind, Sam smiled and drifted off to sleep.

# Chapter Eighteen

## Wyatt

It was one of his long run days, and Wyatt was feeling pretty dang good. He was keeping pace exactly where he wanted to be, and it was much easier than he'd expected after his lax training while in Vail. His running playlist consisted of music at exactly the proper beats per minute to keep his feet hitting the pavement at precisely the correct pace to keep him on track. And while he wasn't a fan of every 150 BPM song on his list, that was irrelevant to the purpose they served. The Pearl Jam song he did like had just ended, and it transitioned into a song his Uncle Bowen had recommended by an '80s hair band called Poison. Wyatt cringed, but he couldn't deny that the tempo was perfect for his pace.

As he strode smoothly in time with the loud drums and screeching electric guitar, Wyatt thought that Sam might like this song, and he wondered if he should share it with him. Sam was into music of all types—he was an incredibly talented singer in his own right—and while Wyatt didn't share his passion in the same way, he admired Sam for his musical knowledge and ability. Sam might not appreciate the song because of its desired 150 BPM tempo like Wyatt did, but he imagined Sam playing air guitar and bouncing around to the vintage rock tune, and that made him smile. He could picture his red hair falling into his eyes as he committed to the motion of the air guitar strumming with the same dedication he brought to his karaoke performances. Yep. Wyatt was going to play this song for him. He had to see it.

The song ended, and a slower tempo song started up, signifying to Wyatt that he was at the cooldown portion of the run. Which made sense. He was two miles from the cafe, and he knew he would be moving from the current 130 BPM Ariana Grande tune to the 110 BPM Queen classic, "Another One Bites the Dust," then the even slower 90 BPM of Sublime, and then he'd be at the cafe. The cooldown went smoothly as well, and by the time he rounded the final corner to end up on the cafe's street, he was breathing deep and even, his heart slowing itself back down to its non-running rate, the sweat cooling on his back and forehead as he slowed his pace to a walk. As much as he was in disbelief, he thought he might actually be in shape for the race, slightly ahead of schedule, despite the setback of the wedding. He mentally scolded himself. He shouldn't think of Matt and Jasper's wedding as a setback. He just meant in terms of his training for the run. But clearly, it hadn't been. Truth be told, he hadn't thought much about running at all while he was in Vail. Not with everything that had transpired between him and Sam. He felt his cheeks flush at the thought, and he was thankful that his blushing could be excused as a natural physiological effect of running because he was at the cafe, and when he pushed the door open, he was greeted with a wave and a grin by his uncle, who was shutting the door to the glass pastry case he'd apparently just filled. "There he is," Bowen boomed. "How's my little Flo-Jo?"

"Is Florence Griffith Joyner the only runner you know of?" Wyatt asked his uncle. "Because that is really showing your age, Uncle Bo."

Bowen flipped Wyatt off before grabbing a plate from the stack behind the counter, opening the pastry case, and using a pair of tongs to retrieve a blueberry scone. He placed it on the plate and slid the plate across to Wyatt. He set an empty glass beside it, which Wyatt took and brought over to the serve-yourself water station on the side of the counter. He took a few big swallows and refilled the glass before returning for his scone. He grabbed the plate and the scone and took a seat at the first small table nearest the counter. The cafe wasn't actually open for business yet. Bowen had a habit of neglecting to lock the door behind him when he arrived for opening duties. Wyatt had told him more than once that that wasn't a safe business practice, but the times Bowen listened to Wyatt were few and far between. Not many were as pigheaded as his uncle.

"So, how'd you do this morning?" Bowen asked, his hands busy behind the counter as he stocked the till's drawer with the proper change for the day.

"Good, actually," Wyatt admitted. "I think I'm ready."

Bowen smiled. "Told you."

Wyatt gave his uncle some side-eye before biting into the scone. Wyatt's smartwatch vibrated with an alert, indicating a text message from a number he didn't recognize. He tapped on the notification, which made very little sense. It was a Google Calendar invite to a Hicks-Olson Security meeting. Weird.

"What's with the furrowed brow?" Bowen had pulled

out the seat across from Wyatt, turning the chair backward and taking a seat. His arms rested on the chair's back.

"I just got a strange text. I think it was sent to me by accident. It's from Hicks-Olson Security."

Bowen raised a brow. "I want to be in the group text with those guys. Just imagine if one of them accidentally sent a dick pic to the group. I bet Hicks is packing like nobody's business. He oozes BDE."

Wyatt scowled at his uncle.

"Seriously, Wyatt, add me to the group chat. I saw Wilkinson eyeing Clark. Maybe he'd be into a threesome..."

Wyatt was the one to flip off his uncle that time.

"Maybe it was meant for Sam?" Wyatt's brain whirred with scenarios in which he would be contacted by the Hicks-Olson team. But that didn't make any sense. Danson had been Sam's personal security long enough to get his number right. In fact, they were a capable security team. They didn't send oopsie texts to wrong numbers. Wyatt would have to follow up and see what this was all about. For the time being, he closed out of the notification and finished his scone. He could deal with that later when he was showered and behind his laptop. It was important for Wyatt to focus on certain tasks at certain times and in certain contexts. Otherwise, it was easy for him to be overwhelmed, and when he was overwhelmed, he was unproductive. And there were few things he hated more than being unproductive.

"How's it going with Sam, by the way?" Bowen looked at Wyatt with what he assumed was supposed to be curiosity, but Wyatt could see concern on his uncle's face from a mile away.

"It's good," Wyatt said, nodding. "I think."

"Oh!" Bowen sat up straight and clutched his heart with

both hands. "Don't throw around that level of enthusiasm all willy-nilly," he said. "My old heart can't take it!"

Wyatt scowled at him. "What do you want me to say?"

"I don't know," Bowen said, no longer caught up in his dramatics. "Maybe you finally getting together with the love of your life for whom you've been pining for years could elicit more than 'It's good, I think.'"

Wyatt shrugged. "I don't know that we're 'together' like that. I mean, we definitely were 'together' in some senses of the word in Vail, and we...you know...said things..."

Bowen narrowed his eyes at his nephew, but he didn't interrupt.

Wyatt continued. "But does that mean we're an official couple now? In Los Angeles? I don't know."

Bowen tilted his head back, facing the ceiling like he was praying for strength. "Please tell me the two of you didn't confess your love, have sex, and then just not talk about whether that meant you're in a relationship. Has Sam met you? Doesn't he know you need explicit confirmation of every little thing? What is this? Amateur hour?"

Wyatt felt his cheeks heat. He hadn't explicitly told his uncle that he'd slept with Sam, but he had told him Sam had said he reciprocates his feelings. Apparently, Bowen had put the pieces together about the physical part of it.

"All I can say, kiddo, is that you need to speak to Sam. Confirm that you're boyfriends and see why his security team is inviting you to meetings." Bowen smirked. "And ask if Wilkinson wants to be the marshmallow in a Bowen and Clark s'more." Bowen got a dreamy look on his face and licked his lips.

"Gross," Wyatt said, but he felt his lips twitch up at the corners. As insufferable as his uncle was, he was a lovable pain in the ass.

"Speaking of gross," Bowen said, standing and righting the chair he'd been sitting in. "Get your stinky hind outta here. You're going to scare off the paying customers." He strode to the front of the cafe and flipped the "open" sign so it faced out.

Wyatt stood, too, bussing his plate and water glass. "See you later," he said, putting his AirPods back in and exiting the cafe. His apartment was walking distance from the cafe, so it was easy for him to go back and forth from the cafe to his place to his office, which was a small space that Bowen rented in the same neighborhood. While Bowen worked mainly from the office in the back of the cafe, Wyatt did his part of running The Price Group from their official office space three blocks over. He didn't have to worry about the beats per minute of his listening material on the way back. He was more of a podcast guy on his walks, always keeping up with the latest in the business world. His uncle was the money behind The Price Group, and Wyatt was the one who protected that wealth, growing and investing it in such a manner that had grown their business significantly over the last five years. Wyatt knew that his uncle greatly preferred stocking pastries and chatting up customers in the cafe that he shared with Matt to doing any of the financial or strategic things that Wyatt took care of, and that suited Wyatt just fine. He was much more of a numbers guy than a people guy, and he was more than content with that.

Wyatt tapped around on his watch, about to start up the latest episode of one of his favorite podcasts when he recalled the notification from Hicks-Olson. He decided to just get it cleared up then, rather than wait. It was likely some simple misunderstanding, and there was no use having to worry about it any longer than necessary. He found the notification and called the number. He heard ringing in his AirPods as he walked toward his apartment. After three rings, he heard, "This is Dan," come through.

"Oh. Hi. Danson?"

"Yes, this is Dan," he repeated.

"This is Wyatt. Wyatt Price. I think you may have mistakenly sent me something this morning."

"No mistake," Dan said. "If you can't make that time, we can be flexible."

"I'm sorry," Wyatt said. "What is this regarding?"

"Didn't Sam speak with you?"

"About what?"

"I'll take that as a no," Danson said. "Sorry for the confusion. Sam was supposed to speak with you."

"About what?" Wyatt felt nerves buzz in his belly. "Is he okay?"

"He's fine," Danson said. "I'll have him call you."

"Uh, okay," Wyatt said. He stood outside his apartment complex, confused.

"Everything's fine," Danson said more gently.

"Okay," Wyatt said.

"Sam'll call you."

"Okay," Wyatt repeated. The call disconnected.

Wyatt's mind was racing. What on earth was going on? Why was Danson trying to schedule a meeting with him? And why hadn't he heard anything about it from Sam? What the hell was going on?

He shook his head and swiped his keycard for access into his apartment building. He dug out the key to his unit, which he kept on the lanyard he wore tucked in his shirt with his building's keycard and his credit card in case of emergencies when he ran. As he was unlocking his apartment door, his watch buzzed with another notification. He glanced at it but couldn't see much of it without tapping into it. But from what he could see, it was from Sam. *Good.* Wyatt exhaled with relief at this whole thing being cleared up sooner rather than later. He opened the apartment door and dropped his key and lanyard on the counter in the kitchen beside his phone, which he'd left there when he was on the run. He picked up his phone and opened the notification from Sam. It was a text message that did the exact opposite of settling the nerves in his belly. It simply read: "I'm sorry. I'll call you when I can."

# Chapter Nineteen

## Sam

Sam quickly put a few of the random socks and hoodies he had strewn around his apartment into his hamper. He'd just finished with a long meeting with the producers from *Ominous*, discussing the "game plan," as they called it, for the upcoming season, which was right around the corner. In fact, shooting began in a few days. It had felt good to be back home in LA, and heading into the *Ominous* offices felt a bit like returning home. As much as Sam had loved his time away while in Colorado, he was also eager to get back to work. He would never take it for granted that he got to make a living doing what he loved. Despite the challenges that came with fame, he truly wouldn't trade it for the world. Playing Caspian had been the opportunity of his life, which he owed in large part to his new brother-in-law and boss, Jasper. So, despite the gnawing feeling in his gut about the conversation he was soon to have, he knew it was necessary, and he would do it. It was part of the cost of getting to live his dream. And, as Clark always told him, those who truly mattered wouldn't be deterred by his circumstances. Sam hoped he was right.

It was five minutes to 7:00, which was when Wyatt was due to arrive. Looking around his space, Sam nodded in approval. It didn't look too bad. That probably had a lot to do with the fact that he'd done little more than wheel his suitcase in, crash, then rush off to his meeting, not having time to create the usual Sam-nado mess that was typically a hallmark of his living space. He messed with the dimmer switches, not wanting to have the lighting too harsh, but also not wanting to make it look like he was trying to set a "mood." They did have important things to discuss, after all. And when that was done, he would worry about the mood lighting. Actually, he thought, maybe they could start with the naked parts, and then have the conversation. He certainly hoped they'd get to the naked parts. It had been many excruciating hours since he'd had Wyatt in his arms. That was partially why he'd insisted that Dan go to his own place for the evening. Sam was home, safe and sound in his apartment, and he really, really needed some alone time with Wyatt. As much as he liked the big guy, Dan was a bit of a boner killer with his ever-present chaperoning. As hot as he was, his mother-hen persona didn't exactly scream "sexy."

Sam glanced at the clock, seeing it was 6:57. If he knew Wyatt, and he was certain he did, he imagined Wyatt waiting in his car in the parking lot until 6:58, having calculated that it would take him just under two minutes to walk in and ride the elevator up to Sam's place. He was odd like that—he was never late, but he also didn't like to arrive anywhere too early. And he had an uncanny ability to calculate exactly how long it took to park and walk into any given venue. Sam, on the other hand, usually ran into wherever he was supposed to be seven minutes late, a half-eaten Pop-Tart in hand, and an apologetic smile on his face. He chuckled to himself at how opposite he and Wyatt were in some ways. He did think, though, that the ways in which they differed provided much needed balance to both of their personalities. And they did have plenty in common where it counted.

Sam went to the bathroom to check his appearance in the mirror. His red hair was messy, but he thought it looked good that way. Like he was a bit of an impish rogue. Or so he liked to fancy himself. He turned his head to one side and then the other, admiring his reflection. Yeah, despite being tired, he still looked damn good. He could admit that. He straightened his T-shirt and flexed his triceps in the mirror. He was lean, but he was in decent enough shape. He leaned his head toward one arm, taking in a deep whiff of himself. He smelled fine, thankfully. He put his hands on his hips and nodded sharply once. He was ready.

At exactly 7:00 p.m., there was a knock on his door. Wyatt was on the doorman's list of "approved visitors" as designated by Danson, so he didn't need to buzz up from the entryway. Sam's belly butterflies took flight as he bounded toward the door. He couldn't wait to see Wyatt.

Sam opened the door, a big, stupid grin on his face, which only stretched wider when he saw Wyatt on the other side, standing there in his shirt and tie, fidgeting with the buttons at his cuffs. His hair was down, tucked behind his ears, and Wyatt gave Sam a small, shy smile, and said, "Hi."

Sam didn't bother with a verbal response. He reached out and pulled Wyatt into his arms, squeezing him and kissing his head. "I missed you," he said into Wyatt's silky hair. Sam's whole body relaxed when he felt Wyatt squeeze him back—not with the same vigor with which Sam used, but it still felt reassuring. Like he was in his rightful place in the world. The way he'd always felt when he was with Wyatt.

Wyatt let out a small chuckle, and his muffled voice spoke from its place pressed against Sam's shoulder. "It's only been two days."

Sam squeezed a bit harder. "Two loooong, painful, lonely days."

Wyatt laughed louder at that, a real, deep, openhearted sound. Nothing had ever sounded so good to Sam.

"So can I come in, or...," Wyatt's muffled voice said eventually.

Sam gave his head one more kiss, his body one more squeeze for good measure, then released Wyatt, gesturing for him to enter the apartment. "Of course, my love. Mi casa es su casa." Sam watched Wyatt closely as he walked in and slipped his shoes off on the mat in the entryway. He grinned when he saw that Wyatt was wearing dress socks with what appeared to be equations on them. "Nice socks, babe," he said.

Wyatt looked down at his feet, as if he had no idea what Sam was talking about, and shrugged. "It's Tuesday."

Sam shook his head, his smile hurting his cheeks. "You still wear specific socks on specific days of the week?"

Wyatt's brows furrowed. "Why would I ever change a foolproof system? Who has time to waste deciding which socks to wear?"

Sam was only about fifty percent sure Wyatt was poking fun at himself, and he loved him all the more for his uncertainty in situations like this. With Wyatt, he was either extremely hilarious with his earnest delivery or just that much of a nerd, and either way, Sam found it extremely adorable.

Sam grabbed Wyatt's hand and led him into the main

living space, stopping by the breakfast bar. "Want something to drink?"

"What do you have?"

Sam pulled Wyatt into the kitchen and opened the fridge with one hand, still hanging on to Wyatt with the other. "Looks like regular water, Pamplemousse sparkling water, or cranberry juice."

"Cranberry juice?" Wyatt raised a brow as he craned his neck to peer into the fridge.

"Mara. She claims it helps her fend off bladder infections or some shit. I try not to ask too many questions when she starts talking about woman problems."

"I'm pretty certain men have bladders too," Wyatt said.

Sam rolled his eyes. "So, you want the cranberry juice then?"

Wyatt smiled. "I'll take the Pamplemousse, please."

Sam let go of Wyatt's hand to retrieve two cans of the sparkling water, passing one to Wyatt and keeping one for himself.

"What would you like me to have stocked for you?" Sam asked him as he led the way to the living room. He sat on the sofa and cracked his can open, Wyatt following behind.

"What?" Wyatt sat and opened his water, too, taking a sip and seemingly waiting for Sam to elaborate.

"What beverages would you like me to stock for you in my fridge? We do a grocery order, and I can get whatever you'd like. Food too. Just let me know."

Wyatt blinked at him a couple of times, and then nodded. "I'm sure whatever is fine. I'm not fussy," he said.

"I know you're not fussy, babe, but what would you like? I want you to want to come here. I want to make it as pleasant an experience as I can," Sam explained. "And while I know I can easily provide the best orgasms of your life, I'd also like to have the proper refreshments for afterward. Or between sessions," he said, grinning like a little devil.

Wyatt set his can down on the coffee table in front of the couch and studied Sam. Sam could suspect, by the look on Wyatt's face, that he was about to get into some serious discussion territory. Certainly, they had things to talk about. And Sam wasn't insensitive to the fact that Wyatt was a worrier. However, he really didn't think he could concentrate on any type of high-stakes conversation with the way his thoughts and his body were imploring him to get to the naked part first. So, before Wyatt could get a word out, Sam leaned forward and took Wyatt's face in his hands and went in for a kiss. It only took Wyatt a second to relax his posture and kiss him back. He hummed and plunged his tongue into Sam's mouth, and Sam's dick perked up immediately at finding Wyatt sharing his enthusiasm for cutting straight to the chase. It just felt so good—being home, having Wyatt there, making out on his sofa. It was exactly what he'd fantasized about countless times since he'd met Wyatt. But in his fantasies, his face was usually buried between Wyatt's thighs. Sam's dick strained at his fly at the dirty thought, and when Wyatt took a nip out of Sam's lower lip, Sam quickly realized it was high time his fantasy fully materialized into reality.

Sam leaned into Wyatt, urging him to lie back on the sofa, Sam following atop him, his mouth eagerly tasting the skin of Wyatt's neck. He lived for the way Wyatt's body shivered when he sucked on just the right spots. "Sam," Wyatt gasped out as Sam ground his hips into Wyatt as he used enough suction to leave a mark at the juncture of Wyatt's shoulder and neck. Wyatt's hands were under Sam's T-shirt, sliding over and gripping onto his sides as Wyatt rocked his hips up into Sam. "Maybe we should talk..."

Sam propped himself up to straddling and loosened Wyatt's tie. Then he went for the buttons of Wyatt's shirt. "Soon," Sam said, as his fingers worked swiftly. "After," he said, as he triumphantly undid the last button and urged Wyatt to help him work the shirt off his body, the tie flung aside with it. "If that's okay with you," Sam said, smirking before wiggling down far enough to tug at Wyatt's undershirt.

Wyatt nodded vigorously, and he lifted his shoulders off the couch long enough for Sam to pull it over his head and toss it aside. "Okay," Wyatt said, closing his eyes as Sam's mouth sealed over his left nipple. When Wyatt let out a small, helpless moan, Sam's balls tightened. If Sam had been worried his head wasn't in the right place when he'd first seen Wyatt, he was in no condition to have a serious talk with his dick aching and Wyatt looking so fucking hot underneath him, making those sexy little moans and whimpers. Sam shimmied down Wyatt's body, settling between his legs, fingers quickly undoing his pants.

"I love the sounds you make," Sam said, making quick work of stripping Wyatt of his remaining clothing. "I feel like the fucking king of the world when you moan like that for me." Wyatt's cheeks were flushed from lust, and maybe a little self-consciousness, but Sam wasn't going to let him feel embarrassed. Every single thing about Wyatt was sexy as hell, and he wanted him to feel confident about that. "I'm serious," Sam continued. He gripped Wyatt just above the knees, forcing his legs apart. He was the one groaning as

Wyatt bent his knees, feet flat on the sofa on either side of Sam, knees wide open and everything on display. "And look at you, babe," Sam said, his voice sounding reverent before he started to trail soft, wet kisses down one of Wyatt's long, slightly trembling thighs. He had dark leg hair, and Sam loved the way it tickled his cheek as he drew his face gently over the places he kissed. "You're so hot when you let yourself relax. Seeing your work clothes in a pile on my floor and your legs spread wide open for me...it's a huge fucking turn on. And I'm still fully dressed." Sam shook his head teasingly. "What a dirty, dirty boy you are." From where Sam sat, he could see Wyatt's hard cock, the head purple and glistening, his balls just begging for his tongue to give them some attention, and below that, Wyatt's tight little hole. "I don't even know where to start," Sam said. "I want to just devour all of you."

To Sam's delight, Wyatt's fingers had found his own nipples, and he was rubbing them between his thumb and finger wantonly, occasionally closing his eyes to hum with pleasure. His hair was a mess, his cheeks pink, and when he opened his eyes to find Sam's, he said, "Then do it. Please."

So, he did. He started with Wyatt's balls, his tongue laving over them both, his hand cupping them to keep them in place while he opened his mouth and hummed on one, then the other. Wyatt had gasped as Sam's mouth rumbled against his sack, and Sam mentally patted himself on the back. Every reaction he earned felt like a gold star, and he swore his dick got a tiny bit bigger with each one he earned. He peeked up to see Wyatt was still fingering his nipples, watching Sam. Sam met Wyatt's eyes before he dipped his head lower, his tongue licking a wet stripe from Wyatt's balls, across his taint, and down to his hole. He just touched the tip to the puckered skin, and Wyatt jerked his hips, and

Sam licked back up. Wyatt's whimper sounded like frustration, and Sam relished that, too. He had his man right where he wanted him. He wrapped a hand around the base of Wyatt's leaking cock and sucked the head into his mouth. He held it there, not working it with his tongue, not jacking him—just holding him in the wet heat of his mouth. Wyatt began to thrust, eager for some friction and movement, and Sam popped off. "I know, baby," he said at the desperate look on Wyatt's face. "But I want to take my time here. I need some lube, okay." He hopped off the couch and jogged down to his bedroom, returning with the lube. "I want to blow you with my finger in your ass, and then, if you can hold off on coming, I'll replace that finger with my tongue, or my cock, or one and then the other, whatever you prefer." Wyatt stared at him with so much emotion in his eyes. Heat. Wanting. Eagerness. Possibly a tinge of frustration and annoyance. All the reactions Sam loved to elicit. "Sound good to you?"

Wyatt's response was to bite his lower lip and resume his nipple play, his eyes drawing Sam back to him like a quicksand, and Sam was ready to be buried. He dove back in between Wyatt's legs, this time going straight for his hole. Sam really wanted to have Wyatt's dick in his mouth, but he figured he'd eat his hole first. He'd swallow less lube that way. He braced Wyatt's legs in place with his hands under Wyatt's knees, and he went for it, sliding the flat of his tongue in Wyatt's crease and over the puckered skin of his hole. "Mmm," he said as he went for another identical pass. He could have sworn he felt Wyatt's hole contract as he tasted it that time, and he looked up at Wyatt. "Do you like that?"

"Yes," Wyatt said quickly. "Very much."

Sam bent down to work in earnest then, circling his

tongue around the rim, getting it sloppy with his saliva. He licked over and over and over, not yet dipping his tongue inside. He wanted to make Wyatt whimper for it first. He pulled his face back, wiping his mouth on the side of his hand. He simply looked at Wyatt for a few seconds, appreciating him, until Wyatt's hands were in his hair, pushing at him to get back to the task at hand. When Sam played clueless for a second and kissed Wyatt's inner thigh, Wyatt finally made the desperate begging sound Sam had been waiting for, and he brought his tongue back to the place Wyatt needed it, and pushed it in. He felt Wyatt's hold tight around his tongue, and he pressed his lips to his hole in a possessive kiss, spearing his tongue in a little deeper. Wyatt was shaking and cursing, and Sam was fucking loving it. His own dick was painfully hard, and he was fully expecting to come in his pants, but that was fine. He could go again if he did. That was the beauty of being twenty-two. He retracted his tongue, swirling it around Wyatt's rim, licking over his entrance, poking it back in. Sam wasn't a rimming expert, but he was sure having fun trying things out. Wyatt's distinct taste, the needy press of his body further against Sam's face, and his moans had Sam speeding up his efforts, going with more vigor. Yeah, he'd had big plans for sucking Wyatt off, but no way was he moving from this spot if it had Wyatt losing it like this.

And lose it he did. Sam was tongue fucking him furiously when Wyatt's hands pulled his hair, and Wyatt let out a strangled cry, and his hole squeezed. Sam kept plunging his tongue in and out, squeezing hard on Wyatt's thighs, as Wyatt lost it. He shot his load all over his stomach and chest, and his legs fell open limply. His fingers were still tangled in Sam's hair when Sam finally pulled out and sat up, appreciating his handiwork. Wyatt lay boneless, spread open, naked, and gorgeous on his couch. His eyes were closed, and his mouth slightly open, his chest rising and falling rapidly as he came down. Sam had never seen anything so gorgeous, and he had never, not once, felt so lucky.

# Chapter Twenty

## Wyatt

Having just recovered from the most intense orgasm of his life, Wyatt still felt a bit unsteady on his feet when Sam suggested they move to his bed for actual sleep. He'd agreed, used the bathroom, put his boxers back on, and gone into Sam's bedroom. Sam went into the bathroom, and Wyatt climbed into Sam's bed. He snuggled into the fluffy white comforter, his head on the pillow, not a care in the world. Sam had just absolutely taken him apart with his clever tongue, and they were together, back in LA, and it felt like all was finally as it should be. Wyatt was sleepy and sex drunk and was only vaguely aware that Sam was taking a while to join him in bed.

Sam crawled into bed beside him a few minutes later. "Sorry," Sam said. "I just had to jerk off really quick. But I'm good to sleep now, if you're tired."

Wyatt smiled, turning to face his beautiful man. Sam had flicked off the lights, but he could still vaguely make out his face in the dark. "Sorry I didn't help get you off," he said, though he knew Sam wasn't mad.

"Don't be sorry," Sam said. "It was a stroke and a half, and I was busting. That whole thing back there," he pointed a thumb over his shoulder toward the door, "that was for me as much as it was for you, my love."

Wyatt's smile widened, and he snuggled up to Sam, the two of them holding each other the same way they'd done in Vail. As Wyatt was drifting off, a thought poked around in his brain, and he mumbled to Sam, "We were supposed to talk." He recalled the security meeting and all the unsettled things between them, and a small kernel of worry sprouted back in his belly.

But Sam simply smoothed his hair down, kissed his head, and said "Tomorrow," and Wyatt was dazed enough to accept that.

\* \* \*

"So, are we really doing this?" The next morning, over coffee on the very sofa they'd had the hot naked time on the night before, Wyatt was ready to talk. His voice was earnest, and Sam sat his mug down on the coffee table, sliding closer to Wyatt and taking his hands. They'd both turned sideways to face one another, with one knee bent on the couch, one leg on the floor. Their hands were clasped together between them. "For real this time?" Wyatt felt so vulnerable asking that, but he needed to know. This had progressed so much faster than he expected, and he needed to know where they actually stood.

Wyatt saw Sam's throat work as he swallowed, and his eyes looked troubled. Alarm bells started to go off in Wyatt's brain. No. There was no way—not after everything that had happened... He took a deep breath. He was probably just defaulting to a worst-case scenario like he always did. He needed to be calm, reasonable, and hear what Sam had to say. Sam ran his thumbs over the skin of Wyatt's hand, like he was gathering his courage. "I hope so," Sam said. "But it won't be easy."

Wyatt looked at him, studying Sam's face. He couldn't tell what Sam was thinking, but Sam forged on. "I want to be with you—for real—but here in LA it will be...different than it was at the lodge. More complicated." He watched Sam's expression closely for any signs of his feelings about what he was saying, but he couldn't tell. Wyatt was simply looking at him, patiently waiting for him to continue. Sam took a deep breath, and Wyatt squeezed his hands, an attempt to reassure Sam that he could talk to Wyatt about anything. Seemingly, it gave him the courage to just spit it all out. "Dan says you need personal security, and I think he's right. I really don't want anything to happen to you, Wyatt. I'd never forgive myself if someone hurt you because of me. And you're going to be in the news. People will say mean things. About you. About me. And you'd have to be okay with that. You won't be able to just be anonymous. And I know that you feel comfortable that way. And that you'd never ask for any of the attention you're going to get." Sam sighed, and Wyatt saw his eyes fill with tears. He looked at Wyatt, a silent plea in them, but for what, exactly, Wyatt didn't know. "I just want you to know what you'd be getting into to be with me. I know it's a lot to ask." Was Sam trying to convince him that they shouldn't be together? Or was he trying to convince him that they should? What the hell was going on?

Sam let out another slow breath, waiting for Wyatt's response. Wyatt had lowered his eyes, seemingly staring at their entwined fingers. He didn't immediately speak, but he felt his guts knot and twist. He didn't ever recall being so nervous or afraid in his entire life. After painfully long seconds, Sam couldn't help himself. "Wyatt?" At Sam's prompt, Wyatt finally looked up at him again, and he felt the tears pooling in his eyes, as well. He squeezed Sam's fingers tighter.

When Wyatt spoke, his voice was quiet, careful. "You know I love you," he said, not sure what else he should really say. Sam's expression seemed pained, and Wyatt wasn't sure why telling him that he loved him made him look that way. It felt like a swift kick to his twisted-up gut.

"But..." Sam said the word before Wyatt could continue. "There's a but, isn't there?" As much as Wyatt wished he could say no, the truth was, there was a but. Sam was right. This wasn't going to be easy. And they had been impulsive, rushing into things. They just loved each other so much, things went from zero to serious in record time. And with Sam being famous, and Wyatt being Wyatt, there were bound to be complications. Wyatt had never even considered that he might need security. Or that he would even get attention apart from when he was out with Sam. They'd been naive. He'd been naive.

Wyatt nodded almost imperceptibly.

At Wyatt's nod, Sam broke. He choked out a sob and the tears ran down his freckled cheeks. It broke Wyatt's heart to see it, and he pulled Sam to him, wrapping him in his arms, squeezing him close while his own tears fell.

"Please don't cry," Wyatt said to Sam. "I'm sorry," he said, holding Sam tightly. "I don't want to hurt you."

Sam's sobs shook his thin frame, and Wyatt's shoulder was damp beneath Sam's face. As much as it was killing him, his resolve grew. Seeing how much power he had over Sam, and knowing full well that Sam had the same hold on him, Wyatt's resolve solidified. They had to do this. He had to do this. After a few fortifying breaths, Wyatt attempted to calm Sam. He ran a hand over the back of Sam's head, smoothing his hair and making the shushing sound Uncle Bo used to use on him when he'd been crying over something. "It's okay, Sam," Wyatt murmured. "It'll be okay."

Sam sniffled and clung to Wyatt, and Wyatt felt Sam's head move from side to side, like he was trying to shake it in disagreement. "No," he said, his voice broken and miserable. "It won't be okay. Not if you're breaking up with me. That is not okay, Wyatt." Sam's arms tightened around Wyatt, like he was holding him until Wyatt took back what he'd been trying to say. The tears fell silently down Wyatt's cheeks, and he let Sam hold him, splaying his hands against Sam's back and closing his eyes, breathing Sam in. Despite the circumstances, it still felt good to be in Sam's arms. More tears fell at the thought, and Wyatt worked to steady his breathing.

This was why they needed to have this conversation. They had too much power over one another. It wasn't safe for either of them. It never had been.

"You're not shutting me out again," Sam muttered, and he pulled back from Wyatt enough to look at him with big, tear-sparkling eyes. "You hear me?" Sam's jaw ticked, and Wyatt saw him gathering his bearings, gearing up for a fight if need be. "You are not shutting me out again, Wyatt. I won't have it." Sam's arms gripped Wyatt's biceps firmly, holding him in place so he had to face Sam.

Wyatt shook his head quickly. "I don't want to shut you out. I wouldn't do that. Never again. I promised you that."

Sam's shoulders relaxed slightly, but he narrowed his eyes. "Then what are you talking about? You made it sound like you wanted to break up with me."

Wyatt lowered his eyes, and Sam brought one hand to

169

his chin, lifting his face so he had to look at him again. "Wyatt. Talk to me. Please. I can't take this. What the hell is going on?"

Wyatt squeezed his eyes closed and took a deep breath. Then he looked up at Sam, the man he loved more than anything on earth, and proceeded to break his heart. "I think we should take a step back," Wyatt said. "Now that we're home. We need to figure out how to move forward in a way that makes sense," he said. Sam looked like he wanted to argue, his mouth opening, but Wyatt cut him off. "Please," Wyatt said. "Please just hear me out."

Sam nodded, dropping his hands from Wyatt's arms. Wyatt reached out and re-laced their fingers together. Sam looked down at their entwined hands, then up at Wyatt's face. Sam's expression looked expectant but sad.

"I don't want to get this wrong," Wyatt said, his eyes imploring Sam to hear the actual words he was speaking and not "I don't want you"—because that was the farthest thing from the truth. Wyatt could see that Sam wanted to interject again, but he held back the impulse, waiting for Wyatt to continue. "The thing is," Wyatt continued, "as much as I love you—and I love you so much, Sam; you know that—I think we rushed into this." He looked down at their joined hands. "We can't go from avoiding one another and barely speaking to me being a celebrity boyfriend who needs a security guard." Sam shook his head, but Wyatt pushed on. "If I've learned anything over the last few months, it's that I need to listen to my gut. And work on putting those needs first. And..." Wyatt's eyes were on their joined hands, and he swallowed hard. He took a deep breath in and released it slowly before speaking again. Sam sniffled, but he didn't say anything. "I need to take a minute," Wyatt said, his voice wavering. "I need to know that if we're doing this, we're doing it right. Because I can't lose you again. No matter what, I know I can't handle that. So, if that means stepping back and taking our time right now—easing into this rather than running headfirst over the cliff—then as much as it kills me, I think we need to...take a minute." Wyatt's cheeks were moist, and he looked at Sam, whose tears were falling again. "I want to be with you more than anything, Sam. But when we do it for real, when we officially take that step, I need us both to be ready. Because there will be no going back for me once we do. Not ever. So, I need for us to do it right."

Silence followed those last words from Wyatt, and Wyatt felt the panic set in. What was he thinking? What had he done? He finally had Sam, the man he loved more than everything else in existence, and he was, what? Pushing him away? Was he trying to get back at him? Just scared shitless and breaking Sam's heart before Sam could break his again? Should he take it back? Could he if he tried? Wyatt opened his mouth to beg Sam to forget all the stupid things he'd just said and rewind to the time Sam had answered the door. They'd have a do-over, and it would all be okay. It had to be okay. Before Wyatt could get a word out, Sam broke the silence.

"You're right."

Wyatt's eyes snapped up to Sam's, seeing a new resolve there. It looked less like misery and more like resignation, and that tore a gouge through Wyatt's chest. Somehow, acceptance was a worse emotion to see on Sam's face than anger could have been.

Sam rubbed his thumbs over the backs of Wyatt's hands, reversing the roles of comforter and comfortee once again. They seemed to do that a lot—flipping their roles until Wyatt was dizzy. "You're right," Sam repeated. "We need to do it right. And if you're not ready yet, I can respect that. I'll wait as long as you need. I'll do whatever it takes for you to feel comfortable being with me." He released one of Wyatt's hands to swipe at both of his cheeks. "I know I deserve this," he said. "That I need to earn your trust."

Wyatt's heart hurt hearing that, and his reflex was to argue that Sam didn't need to earn anything. He wanted to take all the hurt and sadness from Sam, assuring him that it would all be okay. But he couldn't do that. Because Sam was right; Wyatt needed to be able to trust him, and if he was truly honest with himself, there was still a little part of him that just didn't. But he really, really hoped he could in time.

# Chapter Twenty-One

## Sam

It never failed; any time Sam walked onto the film lot, he still felt that indescribable exhilaration like he had the first time he'd stepped foot on the *Ominous* set. It was the same feeling he'd had the time his friend Annabeth had invited him to go to a carnival with her family back in third grade. He'd been the poor orphan kid, so he had never had cotton candy or ridden the Tilt-A-Whirl. And when he'd entered the carnival gates for the first time, the scent of fried food and sugar hitting him, a million colored lights brightening his entire periphery, and the hustle and bustle of the crowd sweeping him up, had him feeling so alive, so happy, and so excited, that feeling had stuck with him. The next time he'd felt it was the first day he'd started working on the show.

It was the first day of filming for *Ominous*'s fourth season, and despite the hammering to his heart he'd just taken, Sam couldn't be more excited. He needed a distraction from the whiplash highs and lows of his emotional rollercoaster relationship with Wyatt. And work was just the ticket. His character, a teenage wizard named Caspian, had gone through the trials and tribulations of fighting the sinister supernatural forces in his small town, all while navigating his life as a queer kid in high school. Sam couldn't be prouder that his portrayal of Caspian was well-received, and it was still surreal to see the TikToks and social media posts from queer kids all over the world who were inspired by seeing the gay character, and Sam—a bi/pan actor—on their TV screens.

"Morning, Sam!" Maeve, one of the PAs on the show, greeted him on his way into hair and makeup. "How was Colorado?"

"It was fantastic," Sam said, giving her a toothy grin as they passed one another. It had been fantastic. All except for the part where they had to come back to LA and Wyatt had hit the brakes on them. But today was a new day, he was back at work, and this was just a minor setback with Wyatt. He'd stayed up all night thinking it over. If Wyatt needed him to prove himself, he could do that. He'd be the best prover that had ever proved. And in no time, Wyatt would be back in his arms, in his bed, and all would be right with the world once again. Or so he kept repeating to himself as his own personal mantra in order to get out of bed, showered, dressed, and to work on time. He couldn't convince Wyatt he was truly ready to be with him if he wallowed and got fired. So, Sam was on a mission. Go to work. Kick ass. Give Wyatt the space he wanted and show Wyatt exactly how ready he was.

Once in hair and makeup, Sam took his old familiar chair. He was greeted with a fist bump by Nathaniel, his favorite makeup artist, who had once again changed his hair. This time, it was frosty silver and shaved short everywhere except the top of his head, the long, shiny strands styled artfully to hang over his forehead in a roguish way.

His dark complexion was smooth and flawless as ever, and shimmery green shadow made his brown eyes absolutely sparkle. He was a gorgeous man and a shameless flirt. So, naturally, he and Sam got along swimmingly. "Someone is bringing it," Sam said, giving Nathaniel a deliberate once-over. "Loving the silver."

Nathaniel preened, striking a pose before waving a hand in a dismissive gesture and laughing. "I see you're still a sweet talker," he said. Nathaniel leaned his willowy frame against the vanity and folded his arms in front of him, taking Sam in. "How you been, Red?"

He and Nathaniel were more than actor and makeup artist. They'd spent countless hours together over the last three years. They were friends. So, he knew he'd give him a bit more truth than he'd shared with Maeve on the way in. "I'm good," Sam said. "Mostly."

Nathaniel perked up at that, his perfect brows arching and his posture straightening. "Aww nah," Nathaniel said. "Do I need to slap a bitch?" He unfolded his long arms and reached for his ears like he was going to pull his hoops out and throw down.

Sam shook his head and grinned. "Nothing like that." Nathaniel didn't look convinced, and he narrowed his eyes at Sam.

"You're gonna tell me everything while I deal with this," Nathaniel said, swirling his hand in front of Sam's face. "You know you still need sunscreen in the cooler months, baby boy. Even in the mountains." He tsked and fussed at the pink spots on Sam's now even more thoroughly freckled cheeks. "I am not gonna tell you again, Sam Deerwood. You protect this pretty face."

"You sound like Big Dan," Sam grumbled.

Nathaniel dabbed something onto Sam's nose and

cheeks with a beauty blender as he spoke. "And where is that big, tasty man this morning?"

Sam smirked. He'd long enjoyed watching Dan blush and squirm under Nathaniel's persistent barrage of flirtatious come-ons. Dan acted like he was indifferent, but Sam suspected even he wasn't immune to Nathaniel's charms.

"Security guard meeting," Sam said. "He dropped me off on set and said the lot's security officers could hopefully do their jobs for one morning."

Nathaniel rolled his eyes at the mention of Dan being Dan. "Okay," Nathaniel said as he rummaged around on the vanity for the correct concealer. He turned to face Sam, leaning in before dabbing at the spots under Sam's eyes with the wand thingy Sam knew had a special name, but he didn't really care enough to learn. "Spill it, Red."

Sam sighed, closing his eyes as Nathaniel worked his magic. "Wyatt was there," he started. Nathaniel was quiet, which was not the man's normal state at all, so Sam knew he was all ears. So, he told him everything. How they'd roomed together, dancing at the reception, confessing their feelings. Much to Nathanial's disappointment, he skimmed over the spicier details, but the implication was clear that things of an amorous nature had certainly transpired. Sam finished by relaying their conversation about their decision to take a few steps back just as Nathaniel was misting Sam's face with finishing spray.

"Well?" Nathaniel set down the spray and folded his arms. "What's the plan now?"

Sam shrugged. "Not sure yet. I figured I'd kind of focus on throwing myself back into work, giving Wyatt his space, and going from there."

Nathaniel shook his head, "Boy, you better be joking."

Sam's posture straightened in defensiveness. "Why?

What's wrong with that plan? What else am I supposed to do?" Nathaniel's brows once again rose nearly to his hairline. He stared at Sam in a way that made Sam want to cower or run out of there. He squirmed a bit, fiddling with the cuff of his sleeve. "I tried laying it all out there. That's what I did in Vail," he argued. "And Wyatt said he wants to pump the breaks. So that's what I'm doing. I don't know what you want me to say." Nathaniel didn't move, and now only one of his brows was arched up in judgment. "Don't give me that crossed arms, judgy brow," Sam said, affronted. "I'm doing what he asked of me. That's all I can do." Nathaniel stood firm. "Right?" Sam stared back at him. "It is, though, right? What else can I do? Fight for him? I already did that. Did you not hear the story I just told you? Push him to be with me if he's not ready? That's an asshole thing to do, and it'll scare him off for good." Nathaniel cocked his head to the side, his brow rising even further. Sam wasn't sure how it could possibly do that. But somewhere in his swirling thoughts, a different possibility took root. "Unless he's testing me?" Nathaniel's eyebrows were still raised, but they'd fallen back in line with one another, a gleam of what looked like encouragement glinting in them. "He could be pushing me away because he's scared," Sam said quietly, more to himself than Nathaniel. "If he distances from me first, I can't leave him again." Sam looked up at his makeup artist, who now wore an expression of sympathy.

Nathaniel unfolded his arms and patted Sam on the shoulder. "You're not just a pretty face, Red," he said. "You've got a good head on your shoulders. And a good heart."

Sam felt warring emotions in his gut. On the one hand, there was hope, buoyant and light and wonderful. On the other, there was dread. Because what if Wyatt was testing him, and he couldn't pass that test? What if he didn't know how to get it right this time? It was likely his last chance. The dread weighed the hope down, settling into a ball at the bottom of his stomach. One way or another, Sam knew he needed to resolve this feeling in his gut. He managed a small smile for Nathaniel. "Thanks, man," he said.

"Anytime."

* * *

After a long but what Sam could only describe as kick-ass day on set, Sam found Dan waiting for him at the lot's security station. Dan said he was back to take Sam home, and he wanted to fill Sam in on some of the details from the meeting he'd had with Hicks earlier in the day.

"Before we do that, Big Guy," Sam said. "You know how I told you Wyatt and I were talking a step back and we didn't need Wilkinson?"

They walked side by side toward Dan's parked SUV. Dan eyed Sam warily. "Yes, I recall."

"Half of that is still true," Sam said. "We don't need Wilkinson. But I'm not letting Wyatt get away."

"Oh?" They reached Dan's vehicle, and they paused their conversation to climb in. Dan didn't immediately start the engine. He seemed to wait for Sam to get to his point before taking off.

"I'm going to fight for him and convince him that we're ready," Sam said. "But he doesn't need his own security. That's too much. We can be together like a normal couple in private. And when we're out together, you'll be there. And Wyatt and I have been friends for years. Fans won't pick up on the fact we're a couple right away, anyway.

They've seen me with him before." Dan's jaw ticked, but he didn't interrupt. "Okay," Sam said. "That's my update. Now let's get out of here, and you can tell me about your meeting over a burger."

Dan looked like he wanted to weigh in on what Sam had just said about Wyatt and their relationship, but he didn't. Instead, he asked, "Where do you want to eat?" Sam suspected Dan was keeping some opinions to himself and might share them later, but it didn't really matter. His mind was already made up, and nothing Dan said could deter him.

The fast-food drive-thru snaked through the parking lot and nearly into the street, and Sam sighed. "I'm too hungry for this, Dan-o. Let's just go in."

Dan pulled into the lot and found the lone empty spot in the corner furthest from the entrance. "I'll run in," Dan said. "What do you want?"

Sam had already unbuckled his seatbelt and was opening the door. "I don't know what I want. I'll come in with you."

Dan looked around the full parking lot. "I don't think that's a good idea. At least let me look around first." Sam leaned back into the vehicle and emerged with a Hicks-Olson baseball cap. He pulled it over his red hair and extended his arms out to his sides in a "See?" motion. He closed his door and strode toward the restaurant's entrance. Dan rushed to his side, eyes hopping from left to right and all around, assessing. He overtook Sam and reached the door first. "I'm going in first," Dan said, his tone leaving no room for argument. He opened the door and stepped just inside. Sam folded his arms across his chest and waited.

"You know, if I was going for incognito, you acting like you're the SWAT team isn't helping matters."

Dan grumbled something and entered the restaurant, finally allowing Sam to enter behind him. Despite the full parking lot, the place was only about half full, with a good mix of teenagers, families, and lone adults ordering, eating, and milling around waiting for their food. No one seemed to be paying them any attention as they approached the counter. Sam scanned the menu, taking his time. He was fortunate enough to have a fantastic metabolism, and unlike lots of his costars, he really didn't watch what he ate at all. His brothers told him that he needed to be careful because it would catch up with him one day sooner or later, but that day hadn't arrived yet.

"You know what you want?" Sam looked at Dan, who was still sweeping the entire place with his Dan-o-Vision.

"Not hungry," Dan said.

"Come on. Eat something. My treat."

"I'll have a burger," Dan said.

"What do you want on it? Lettuce, tomato, and mayo? Pickles and mustard? Fries for a side? Or onion rings? I know how you like your onion rings. Come on, Dandelion. At least look at the menu." Dan glared at the back of Sam's head as Sam stepped up to the waiting cashier to place his substantial order. But when Sam turned back to Dan, Dan begrudgingly stepped up to place his order with the cashier. The cashier handed Sam a number, and Sam went off in search of an empty table just as Dan tried to tell her it was to go.

"Hey!" Dan said over his shoulder to Sam as he took the cup the cashier was handing him. "Hold up."

But Sam had already turned the corner. And that was a mistake.

# Chapter Twenty-Two

## Wyatt

Wyatt felt his watch vibrate, and he glanced at the display, seeing his Uncle Bowen's name. He was finishing up his cooldown after the last long run of his training regimen. He'd made it the eight miles at a comfortable pace, and over the next four days, he'd be resting or running short, easy distances to allow his body to be in top shape for race day. He slowed to a walk and answered the call. "Hey," Wyatt said.

"Wyatt," Bowen said, his tone one that immediately had Wyatt's hackles rising. After not only living with his uncle for the better part of his life, but also working with him closely, he knew his uncle's various tones of voice. His default was jovial or teasing. This was neither. He sounded serious, possibly upset. "Where are you?"

"Just finishing a run," Wyatt said.

"Can you come to our place?"

"What's going on?"

"We can talk when you get here," Bowen said.

"You're freaking me out," Wyatt said, quickly turning on his heel and quickening his stride as he made his way toward Bowen and Clark's. "Just tell me what this is about." Wyatt could hear whispering on Bowen's end of the phone, like voices were speaking in the background, but he couldn't make any of the words out.

"Just get here," Bowen said. "It's Sam."

That was all Wyatt needed to hear. He ended the call and started running again.

* * *

"What happened?" Wyatt said the second Bowen answered the door. "Where's Sam? How is he?"

Bowen's hair was a mess, and his eyes were hard. He looked like he was nearly as worked up as Wyatt felt. "He's here," Bowen said. "In the living room." Bowen held the door open for Wyatt, who rushed past him, finding Sam in the middle of the sofa, Clark, Matt, and Mara all piled on either side of him, Danson pacing in front of the glass doors that led out to the balcony.

"What happened?" Wyatt spoke the question to the room in general. He didn't give a shit who responded, as long as someone did, and fast.

Sam looked up at him, eyes wild, tear streaks on his cheeks. "Wyatt," he said in a trembling voice.

Wyatt rushed to him, and since there was no place on the sofa beside Sam, he knelt at his feet. Wyatt placed his hands on Sam's knees and searched his face. "What happened? Are you okay? What's going on?"

Sam looked like he wanted to speak, but instead, he broke into a sob, and grabbed for Wyatt. Wyatt opened his arms and pulled him into a tight hug, squeezing Sam to him, rage building in his gut for whomever or whatever had upset Sam so much. Wyatt ran his hand up and down Sam's back and shushed him soothingly. "It's going to be okay," he murmured as Sam cried into his shoulder. Wyatt had no idea what was even wrong, but he knew for certain he would make it okay. That or he'd die trying.

Wyatt held Sam, who clung to him. Sam sniffled, and he said, "You're right." He sounded absolutely dejected.

"I was right about what, babe?" Wyatt continued smoothing his palm along Sam's back, aiming to soothe him, but it clearly wasn't working.

Sam pulled back enough to look at Wyatt with a wrecked expression. "They had the shoes."

Wyatt was trying to make sense of that, but he just couldn't. He searched his brain for any possible meaning there could be to that phrase, but he kept coming up empty. "What shoes?"

"The shoes!" Sam said, what little composure he'd gained from Wyatt's presence evaporating to dust. "They were all wearing the shoes, Wyatt! And they think I'm having an affair with Dan. They had so many photos. How did they get them? I don't understand. But you were right." Sam nodded and wiped his nose on his sleeve, which Wyatt let pass because Sam was so distraught. "It was stupid to think we could just jump into this. How could I have even thought that? Like this"—he gestured wildly to himself and the whole room—"wouldn't blow back on you. And you hate crowds and drama and the unexpected. How could I do that to you? How could I have ever asked that of you?"

Wyatt was struggling to keep up with the words Sam was spewing from his mouth, but he could certainly register Sam getting more and more agitated again, and he needed to calm him down. He gripped both of Sam's biceps and said, "Look at me. Breathe, Sam. Slow down. Just breathe."

Together, they took a few deep, slow breaths in and out,

until Wyatt was satisfied that Sam's heart rate had slowed back down to a manageable pace. Wyatt was also aware that no one else in the room was intervening in what was happening, but they were all still there, watching Sam in concern. It was like they trusted that Wyatt was the best person to try to talk Sam down from whatever the hell was happening.

"Now," Wyatt said, his voice firm but careful, "I'm going to ask someone else to tell me what happened so you can just work on your breathing." He stared at Sam, and Sam nodded, taking in another shaky breath and holding it a few seconds before expelling it the way Wyatt had been doing with him moments before. "Good," Wyatt said, managing a small smile that he hoped was encouraging.

Keeping one hand's fingers laced with Sam's, Wyatt turned toward the person he thought most likely to explain the situation in a clear, rational manner. "Danson?"

Danson stopped his pacing and crossed his arms over his wide chest. "I didn't let anyone near him," Dan said, steel in his voice. "And they're lucky they didn't push me one step further." There was murder in his voice, sending a chill down Wyatt's spine. While logically he knew Danson was a hard-ass bodyguard, all his interaction with the man had also proven him to be articulate, respectful, and kind. So, seeing the rage bubbling just beneath the big man's surface was extremely unsettling.

"What happened?" Wyatt figured he better ask simple, direct questions because he was beginning to lose his shit about not knowing anything about why the love of his life was a shaking, tear-soaked mess on the sofa.

Danson seemed to take a steadying breath, and his eyes went to Sam, as if checking that he would be okay if Danson recounted the incident. Sam gave a small nod as he continued the exaggerated motions of sucking air in to fill his chest and blowing it out. His fingers tightened on Wyatt's hand when Danson told the story.

"We were at the burger joint off Forty-Sixth, and the drive-thru was busy. Sam wanted to just go in, and he wouldn't let me go for him. I told him to wait in the car." Dan shook his own head, as if to dismiss that. "It was obviously my fault. When it comes to safety protocol, I should certainly be able to stand my ground. I'm the fucking bodyguard, after all," he said, clearly more to scold himself than to further the story. "Anyway," he continued, "we went inside and ordered. I was grabbing the table tent when Sam rounded a corner to snag a booth." Danson ran his hands through his hair, which was a gesture Wyatt hadn't recalled seeing from him before. He was clearly rattled. "And there was a group of people there eating. They saw Sam and immediately recognized him." Danson swallowed hard, and Sam squeezed Wyatt's fingers. "When I came up behind Sam, they were already firing questions. Apparently, they had somehow known which shoes he'd been wearing to run in Vail, and they were all wearing them. They were asking him personal questions about his time in Colorado, and they knew scary amounts of detail." Dan's steely eyes landed on Wyatt. "They asked for selfies with him and me, saying they knew he was sleeping with his 'bodyguard,' and they used finger quotes and one of them winked like it was a joke. The rest of them laughed and started talking about seeing the photos of us in suits walking into the wedding venue together."

Wyatt felt his eyes widen, shocked that there could have possibly been so much detailed information about their time in Vail available on social media already, especially since Wyatt hadn't seen a single paparazzo anywhere. How did they know this stuff? How did they have photos? Everyone at the wedding was family or friends. It didn't make sense.

"When Sam said he couldn't do photos, one of the guys got angry. He started to say…" Danson looked down at his feet and then up at Sam. His eyes were pained when they flicked back over to Wyatt. "He started to say some unkind things about Sam. And his acting, and…his family." Danson mumbled the last part.

Mara wrapped her arm around Sam and spoke up next. "I don't care what they say about me. They can call me his whore sister all they want. I don't care. It doesn't bother me."

"Wait…" Wyatt looked to Mara next. "They were speaking rudely about you? Why?"

"Because of my relationship, I guess," Mara said. "There were photos of Tyson, Harlow, and me at the wedding. Calling me a degenerate and a slut and saying Milo should be taken into protective custody because of our 'disgusting lifestyle.' They can go fuck themselves," she concluded.

"Why would anyone…" Wyatt couldn't wrap his head around that. Sure, Tyson and Harlow were stage actors, but they weren't famous. And Mara was a regular private citizen. It made no sense why people would be so curious and needlessly, ignorantly cruel.

"Because she's my sister," Sam said dejectedly. "And anyone associated with me is apparently fair game to attack if I don't want to take a selfie or sign an autograph. I can take it if they want to call me a bad actor or overrated or whatever. But I can't stomach them going after my loved ones for no reason at all."

Wyatt closed his eyes against the sting of tears threatening to fall. There it was. Sam was rightfully shaken by people's lack of boundaries about him and his family. And Wyatt didn't blame him. It was disturbing how quickly they discovered information and how voraciously they ran with it, whether it was to purchase the same shoes Sam wore or to make up rumors about Sam and Danson having an affair or to slander Mara and her partners for the pure enjoyment of being mean. And now Sam was agreeing with Wyatt that they needed to take a step back because he didn't want to bring Wyatt under that microscope. It was all making sense. And Wyatt hated it.

"I'm so sorry," Wyatt said, directing it toward all of them—Danson, Mara, and especially Sam. It was frightening and heartbreaking. Just because Sam was a celebrity didn't give people the right to have as much access to him as they wanted. It certainly didn't make it okay to attack his family.

"Me too," Sam said, fresh tears streaming down his face again. "I'm so, so sorry."

# Chapter Twenty-Three

## Sam

S am felt sick to his stomach. His alarm had gone off at seven that morning, and it took all his strength to dig himself out of his protective blanket burrow and get out of bed. But despite feeling like absolute shit, he had to go to work. A fresh wave of guilt hit him that he was dreading going to work. At a job that he had dreamed of and genuinely loved. Where he was paid an unbelievable salary and admired all his coworkers. He felt more than ungrateful. But his job was also what was costing him his peace, and worse—the peace of those he loved.

He went to the bathroom and turned on the water in the shower, his gut twisting at the reminder of the things those people had said about Mara. His sister might piss him off like no other, but she was the kindest, most generous and thoughtful person Sam knew, apart from Wyatt. She didn't deserve to be judged or even spoken about by random strangers. She hadn't asked for that, and Sam felt terrible that he'd brought that upon her. He stepped into the shower and immediately immersed his head under the stream of hot water, letting it soak his hair, hit his shoulders and back, and slide down his body. When he closed his eyes, he saw images of those people wearing the running shoes he'd worn in Vail, when he hadn't known there was anyone taking photos of him. The thought of people watching him when he'd been jogging with Wyatt made him equal parts furious and terrified. If Sam was honest with himself, he loved being a celebrity most days. He'd always liked attention, and he had dreamed of being a TV star ever since he first saw Frost Manor and became enamored of Grayson Winter, the show's dashing star, and the whole concept of being part of a world like that. But the last person on earth who would share that feeling was Wyatt. Hell, Wyatt had been uncomfortable with the crowded lodge of friends and family in Vail. He was overwhelmed by too many people at once, and he didn't seem to give a rat's ass about how famous some of the people in their party were. Sam had been an absolute moron for thinking that he could just be with Wyatt like it was no big deal. It would destroy Wyatt's peace of mind. And Sam loved him too much to do that, as much as it killed him to step away.

He washed his hair and body efficiently, not jerking off with the suds for the first time since he could remember. Even his crazy-high libido was subdued by the events of the previous day. He usually pictured Wyatt while he did his morning rubdown, and thinking about Wyatt that morning just caused his chest to ache. He turned off the water and grabbed the towel from the hook. He dried off his hair half-heartedly and stepped onto the bath mat. The mirror was fogged up, and Sam figured that was for the best. He didn't want to know how tired he looked. Nathaniel would certainly have his work cut out for him in the chair that day. Sam ran the towel over his arms and legs and groin, then tied it around his hips. He exited the bathroom and went into his walk-in closet. He normally had a moment of giddiness when he stepped into the massive closet with more clothing than any one guy would ever need. He had actually pinched himself on more than one occasion upon stepping foot into the glorious space. But it didn't feel the same as it often did. This time, he felt sad. He had all the material things he'd ever dreamed of, but at what cost?

Sam sighed and pulled on a pair of Calvins, worn jeans, and a plain green T-shirt. He didn't have the energy to care what he wore to set that day. He wandered back into the bathroom, going through the motions of putting on deodorant, running a comb through his hair, and slapping on his SPF 30 moisturizer. He just couldn't muster up the desire to spritz his cologne or add any product to his hair. They'd just change it when he got to hair and makeup anyway, so what did it matter? And he certainly wasn't going to be making any stops in public on his way into work. Definitely not right now, considering everything. So, the only person who would see his shlubby ass before he got to work was Dan. And Dan wouldn't judge him.

The thought of Dan made Sam's gut churn, too. That was another layer of his guilt. Dan blamed himself for Sam's meltdown the previous day. He kept saying that if he'd been doing his job properly, that would have never happened. Sam had tried to assure him that he hadn't done anything wrong, and that he had protected Sam perfectly. No one had gotten close enough to Sam to touch him, and Dan had safely ushered him out of that restaurant. It wasn't in Dan's job description to protect Sam from things people said or if they were filming with their cell phones while Sam was in public. No one could do anything about that. Sam sighed as he dug a pair of socks out of his dresser and leaned against his bed to pull them on. He would need to reiterate that to

Dan as soon as he got there to pick him up. He couldn't have the big guy blaming himself for Sam being an idiot and freaking out over something that was absolutely part of the territory of being famous.

A fresh wave of nausea hit Sam as he thought about how quickly his "fans" had turned on him when he'd declined to take photos. The horrible things they'd said about Mara were like a punch to the gut, a rude awakening about the realities of the life he'd chosen. Sam wiped his hands over his face, trying to shake himself out of the icky feeling. God, what if they'd said something horrible about Wyatt? How would he have reacted? He was pretty sure the next headline about him would be accompanied by his mugshot. Sam was forced out of his moment of wallowing in despair by the sound of his apartment door opening. A glance at the clock told him that it was 8:15, and Dan was right on time. He took a deep breath in and exhaled slowly, preparing to face Dan with more reassurance not to beat himself up about the incident.

When Sam left his bedroom and entered the hallway, he heard Dan's voice arguing with someone, and Sam wondered if he was on the phone with Hicks. It wouldn't have been the first time that the head of their security team had called Dan bright and early with some update or another. Dan never shared the details of those updates with Sam, and Sam started to suspect they were likely things he'd rather not know. But then another voice—a familiar one—hit Sam's ears. "I'm sorry, Danson. But I don't care if you've got a schedule to keep. This is important."

Wyatt? Sam sped up as he made his way toward his kitchen, where a weary Dan and an agitated Wyatt were in some sort of a face-off. "What's going on?" Sam addressed both men, not caring who spoke first, just hoping someone filled him in quickly. He didn't have the emotional energy to even begin to guess what was going on. Dread was swirling in his belly already. Both men turned to him, and Dan sighed, gesturing helplessly toward Wyatt.

"He needs to speak with you, apparently," Dan said. "He followed me up here and demanded that he see you." Dan glared hard at Wyatt. "And if he wasn't on your approved list of 'admit anytime' people, you'd better believe I would have turned him away because we have somewhere to be."

Sam eyed Wyatt, who stood with his hands on his hips, chin held high, defiant and determined and adorable. "What's going on, Wyatt?"

Wyatt shot some side-eye at Dan, which Sam had never seen him do before, and then marched over to Sam. He stopped a few feet away, and Sam couldn't figure out what was happening. Wyatt was clearly angry, and Sam couldn't make sense of that. When he'd seen Wyatt the night before, Wyatt had been gentle and soothing and calm. Now, he looked damn near belligerent. "What's going on?" Wyatt seemed affronted by the question as he repeated it. "What's going on?!"

Sam was taken aback by Wyatt all hopped up like this. He was the most mild-mannered person Sam had ever known. Aside from when he drank too much, which caused him to get a bit silly, Wyatt was always soft-spoken. "I see that you're upset," Sam started.

"You're damn right I am, Sam!" Wyatt's wide eyes flamed. "You don't get to do this. Absolutely not. Not this time!"

Sam drew his brows in. He was confused. "Don't get to do what?"

"Push me away. Call it off. You don't get to do it, Sam. I don't accept it. It's not happening."

Sam ran a hand through his hair. "Wyatt. You were the one who said we needed to take a step back. You needed your space. Then I realized why that makes perfect sense. I don't live a normal life, and you wouldn't either, if you were with me. I simply agreed with you. After what happened yesterday, I could see it. You'd hate being in the spotlight like that. You'd be miserable. And I can't ask you to do that."

Wyatt's hands were still on his hips, his jaw clenched. He raised one hand and pointed at Sam aggressively. "No." He shook his head. "Absolutely not. You do not get to do this."

"I'm just following your lead, Wyatt." Sam was desperate for Wyatt to see how this was the last thing he wanted, but there was really no other way. Sam had already put him through too much.

"I freaked out when we got back to LA because I was scared," Wyatt said, still angry but his voice slightly softer. "I was pushing you away because I was so scared of what would happen if I lost you again. But it was just me being scared."

"Wyatt..."

"No." Wyatt held a hand up to halt Sam. "You are not to speak until I'm done. You need to hear this." Sam glanced at Dan, who was trying like hell to creep down the hall without being noticed. Wyatt followed Sam's gaze and snapped at Dan. "You stay there, Danson. You can listen to this, too." Wyatt looked into Sam's eyes. "Sam Deerwood, you are not leaving me again. I choose you. I love you. I know you love me too. And you are going to choose me, for fuck's sake!" He spoke with such fervor, Sam was stunned into silence. "I don't care if you're more famous than Taylor

Swift herself. You're not pushing me away. And when I freak out and get scared, you need to prove to me that you won't run. You owe me that. I was absolutely broken when you left me the first time." His voice wavered, and Sam wanted to interject, but Wyatt held up his hand again, and Sam didn't interrupt. "I started running because I was devastated, and I needed to do something. I thought that maybe if I ran far enough and fast enough, I could make it stop hurting. I could move on. But that's the thing, Sam. There is no moving on. Because we're meant for each other. And it is never going to be easy for me. And it sure as hell will never be easy for you. But we don't give up, because we're soulmates. I'm tired of denying that. And I won't let you deny it either."

Wyatt let out a heavy breath, and silence filled the space. Sam didn't know what to do besides look at the face of the man he loved more than anything and let the tears run down his cheeks. He wasn't sure if he was crying because he was sad or hopeful or just so in love his body couldn't contain it. "Wyatt...," Sam started again, his voice a choked sound.

Wyatt interrupted. "You'll be at my race on Saturday, Sam. I trained for it as a way to cope with the loss of you, but now I know that I was training to show myself my own strength. That I can stand up for what I want. That I can tackle any challenge, as long as I know the result is worth it. So, when I cross that finish line, I will see you there." Wyatt looked at Dan and nodded, as if making sure Danson knew that it was an order to be followed as well. Then Wyatt turned and left, leaving Sam stunned.

# Chapter Twenty-Four

## Wyatt

Wyatt avoided looking at his watch. It was something he'd taught himself not to do at any point when he felt himself struggling. Normally, somewhere around mile two, he broke through the mental barrier, and he got into his running zone. When he was in the running zone, his mind cleared, or if not cleared, it decluttered significantly. He was aware of things like the impact reverberating up his legs when his feet hit the pavement or the slight breeze swaying the branches of the trees beside the road. During this particular run, he was also aware of the crowds of people along the route, cheering on his fellow half-marathoners with shouts and handmade poster board signs that he couldn't read as he ran by. He itched to check his watch, to see some inkling of if he was keeping the proper pace or even how far he was into the 13.1 miles, but he didn't dare. He knew it was too early, and looking at those numbers would be discouraging. What he needed to do was drown out the crowds and the other runners and focus on putting one foot in front of the other. He'd keep his eye on the path in front of him and keep pace with the carefully curated soundtrack playing through his earbuds.

The last few days leading up to the race had been difficult. Hell, the whole last week had been an emotional gauntlet he wasn't sure he'd run completely through at this point. It began with the crash from the high he'd been on in Vail when he'd returned to LA. He'd panicked, and he'd tried to push Sam away. He'd tossed and turned in bed that whole night after Sam left, knowing he was just being a coward, and he fully planned to apologize to Sam for his freak-out and ask him to give their relationship a real go of it. And then Sam had had his own meltdown after the incident at the fast-food place. Wyatt couldn't fully comprehend why Sam was so terribly shaken by some questionable "fans," but the fear in Sam's eyes had been heartbreaking. Wyatt had never seen him that way. So, when Sam had been so distraught and told Wyatt that he'd been right, that they shouldn't jump into a relationship, Wyatt hadn't argued. He'd simply held Sam until he'd fallen asleep, and the next morning, Danson had taken Sam to work, and Wyatt hadn't seen him since.

Wyatt had texted, asking Sam how he was and if he could see him, but Sam had brushed him off. He'd said he was "doing better," and "really busy with work," and Wyatt had accepted that. At first. But as the days and hours ticked by, and Wyatt had time to think, he'd had a change of heart. He wasn't going to let Sam off that easily. He wasn't insensitive to Sam's fear from that encounter, but it wasn't something Sam would ever be rid of. At least not any time soon. So, if Sam had to deal with that anyway, why couldn't Wyatt be there for him when he did? Sam's life was public, but Wyatt loved him. And if that meant that Wyatt's life would be public, too, so be it. He was a grown man who could make his own decisions. And he had decided on Sam, and if Sam thought he could push him away under the guise of "protecting" Wyatt, he had another thing coming. So, Wyatt had barged into Sam's apartment one morning, steamrolling Danson and laying it all out for Sam. He told Sam in no uncertain terms that they would not be going their separate ways—that they were going to be together. He'd demanded that Sam come to his race, and that he give them the proper chance they both deserved. And now he was here, running along the blocked-off road, thousands of people in the crowd, hoping beyond hope that Sam Deerwood was one of them.

At Mile 7, Wyatt was supposed to look for his Uncle Bowen and Clark, who would be camped out there until Wyatt came through, before hopping in their car to wait at the finish line for him. Bowen had said it was because he thought his nephew seeing his uncle's "supportive, devastatingly handsome" face halfway through the race would give him the push he needed to make it the rest of the way. Wyatt had rolled his eyes, but he was secretly looking forward to spotting his uncle and Clark in the crowd.

At what Wyatt recognized as Mile 3 of the route, there were large groups of spectators lining either side of the route—dozens of people holding up signs and cheering on their runners. While Wyatt knew that his uncle and Clark were camped out at Mile 7, he couldn't help scanning the crowd for their familiar faces. Clearly, he wasn't quite in the running zone he needed to reach if he was going to make it another 10.1 miles. Just as he was about to focus his attention on the number on the back of a woman a few paces in front of him, effectively "putting his head down" and focusing, someone in the crowd caught his eye. It was a tall man, easily a head taller than those surrounding him, wearing a black baseball cap. Now, a tall guy in a ball cap wasn't anything out of the ordinary, except this particularly tall drink of water seemed to be staring intently at Wyatt. He had dark, hawklike eyes that bored into Wyatt as he jogged past him, and while Wyatt couldn't be entirely certain, the man was eerily reminiscent of a mean Keanu Reeves. Before Wyatt had too much time to dwell on whether that was actually Wilkinson, the personal security officer colleague of Danson's, in the crowd at Mile 3, and if so, why he was there, Wyatt had passed him by. Really, Wilkinson could presumably just be cheering on a family member, friend, or acquaintance. And maybe it hadn't even been him. The whole crowd was kind of a blur as he'd passed them, and maybe he just resembled Wilkinson. Hell, maybe it was actually Keanu Reeves. Wyatt smiled at that idea, and he charged forth into Mile 4.

Somewhere between Miles 3 and 4, Wyatt hit his stride. Maybe it was the Macklemore that he would not be embarrassed about listening to that finally did the trick, or maybe he was just letting his mind fall into the familiarity of his lungs and muscles working together to propel him along a route. In any case, he'd finally hit the zone. He wasn't thinking about his pace or Keanu Reeves or even Sam. His mind was clear, and his heart thumped along as his footfalls on the pavement kept pace with his music. There was definitely something to the theory of a "runner's high." Wyatt was never a drug user, and he was a miserable lightweight when it came to drinking. But running gave him those feel-good vibes that were so elusive to his anxious mind during the daily grind of life. So, while he'd initially started running as a feeble attempt to flee his heartbreak over Sam, he truly had found value in it for his overall well-being.

As Wyatt rounded a corner on the route, he could see in the distance the crowd that had gathered at Mile 7. And holy shit—had he already reached the halfway point? Wyatt searched the crowd, but it didn't take long for him to spot his uncle, who was decked out in a ridiculous approximation of running gear. He'd texted Wyatt a mirror selfie that morning when he'd wished him good luck, and Wyatt had truly hoped the outfit had just been a bad joke. But no. There was his Uncle Bowen in all his glory. He wore the shortest, tightest red shorts known to man with a rainbow-colored tank top. His arms were extended over his head, where he held half of a massive, two-person pink sign that read, "My nephew finishes hard." Wyatt didn't understand why the hell he'd chosen that of all slogans, but he couldn't help but grin. His smile only widened when he saw that on the other side of the sign was Clark, dressed in a pair of khaki shorts and a blue polo shirt, looking none too amused, but dutifully holding up his end of the sign. They were such an adorable, odd couple. Wyatt felt a strong surge of love and gratitude for the both of them for being so supportive and loving. He knew he was lucky to have them. He managed to wave at them quickly as he passed, and even over the music in his earbuds, he could hear his uncle hooting and hollering. Wyatt would never admit it to Bowen but seeing them there did give him a highly welcome boost as he headed into the back half of the race.

Wyatt felt strong and steady for a while through Mile 7. He did start to feel the fatigue setting eventually, however. If he let his mind wander to the race, how his body was feeling, or his pace, he would start to feel the burning in his lungs or his calves. There were blisters on his feet, he was certain, despite all the precautions he'd made. And once, in a moment of weakness, he'd glanced at his watch. He was just under his goal pace, and he still had far too many miles to run. He started to feel the anxiety creep in. What if he was the last person to stumble across the finish line with bloody feet and ready to pass out? What if he didn't even finish the race? What if Sam didn't show? Or worst of all, what if Sam was waiting at the finish line that Wyatt would never cross? The longer he let himself ponder the worst-case scenarios, the heavier his feet felt and the hotter the flames in his throat. There were volunteers along the route with water, so he angled his path to the side to take one of the small paper cups and down it. It wasn't much water—certainly not enough to quench his thirst—but the cool liquid felt good in his mouth.

The stretch between Miles 11 and 12 was brutal. That was the only way to describe it. No fewer than twenty times did Wyatt consider just plopping down on the road and dying. He could just lay right there until the coroner came to drag his carcass out of the street. Why did anyone do this to themselves? And willingly? For fun? What kind of sadist would distance run as a hobby? Near the end of the twelfth mile, an older gentleman that had been keeping pace a few yards ahead of Wyatt stepped to the side of the road and hunched over, his hands on his knees. The man was in fantastic shape, from all appearances, and Wyatt had over-heard him talking with someone earlier about how this was his ninth half-marathon. But he didn't look so good, and while Wyatt knew there were volunteers, and he also knew that stopping would not be a good idea, he couldn't help himself. When he reached the man, he jogged in place beside him. "You okay?" Wyatt asked.

The man's back was rising and falling with his heavy breaths. "Yeah," he huffed. "I just. Need. A minute."

He didn't sound good, and Wyatt searched the sidelines for someone to help. In addition to volunteers and police officers dispersed along the route, there were also medical professionals on hand. He couldn't see any of the volunteers in their teal T-shirts, but he did see a police officer on the other side of the route. She was speaking to someone, so her back was turned to Wyatt and the man, but he called out to her, "Officer? Excuse me, officer?" She turned and immediately wove her way through the runners to reach them. The person she'd been talking to also followed her over to their side of the route, and Wyatt did a double take. It was Hicks. The head of the security firm. The guy who'd been in charge of the personal security for the celebrities at the wedding. While the police officer spoke to the older man who was still hunched over, Hicks addressed Wyatt.

"Everything alright? You doing okay, son?"

Wyatt was so confused and exhausted that he didn't really know how to answer that. Instead of responding to Hicks, he checked in with the man and the officer. She was escorting him to the side of the route and had already radioed for medical assistance. She waved off Wyatt's offer to stay with the man. "Keep going," she said to Wyatt. "You've only got a mile left."

That sparked something in Wyatt. He felt so bad for the man that he'd had to stop running with only a mile left, and Wyatt genuinely hoped he just needed a breather and would be cleared to finish out the race, even if he had to walk the last mile. But hearing the officer say out loud that there was only one mile remaining, Wyatt knew he could do it. He was about to start jogging again when he realized Hicks was still there.

"What are you doing here?" Wyatt said.

"Keeping an eye on things," Hicks said.

Wyatt didn't have time for riddles. "Well, I have a race to finish, so..."

Hicks eyed him. "If you're okay?" he asked one more time.

"I'm fine," Wyatt said, his confusion turning to agitation. Didn't the man see Wyatt was running here?

Hicks nodded, and Wyatt took off, ready to tackle the last mile.

# Chapter Twenty-Five

## Sam

Sam possessed many wonderful qualities; patience wasn't one of them. He'd been jittery all day, and who knew how much longer he'd have to wait. Danson certainly wasn't any help. "How much longer?" Sam asked Dan for the millionth time.

"Hicks says he stopped along the route," Dan replied. He adjusted his black ball cap and stared straight ahead at the finish line as half-marathoners crossed in triumph or tears.

"What? He stopped? Why? Is he okay?"

Dan placed a hand on Sam's shoulder and gave him the be-quiet-or-you'll-blow-your-cover look he'd honed over his tenure as Sam's bodyguard. "He stopped to check on someone who was struggling to breathe. Apparently, the guy's fine, and Hicks says Wyatt's back on the route. He should be here in a couple of minutes."

Sam adjusted his black sunglasses, which kept sliding down his nose. He was annoyed that Dan had insisted he wear a different pair than his usual aviators, but then again, after the incident at the burger joint, Sam was no longer putting up a fuss about any of Dan's precautions. That's why he'd agreed to have the whole damn security team spread out over the route of the race. Surely, it was overkill. Even with how shaken up Sam had been a few days ago, he didn't think it was necessary to have the best and brightest bodyguards in LA all focused on him and Wyatt at a race that was full of police officers. But, if Sam had learned anything over the last month, it was that he didn't really know shit about shit.

Sam bounced on the balls of his feet, unable to keep the nerves at bay. So far, no one had given him or Dan a second glance, and he didn't want to do anything to call extra attention to himself. He was dressed in a black T-shirt, jeans, a black ball cap, and dark glasses. The crowd was focused on the runners, as they should be, and hadn't seemed to notice him at all. Which was a relief. "Do you think he saw Wilkinson or Hicks on the route?"

Dan grunted something, and Sam prodded.

"What was that, Danny Boy?"

"I said he saw Hicks."

"What? Did he blow our cover? If that old goat ruined the surprise, I'm..."

Dan chuckled. "Please let me be there when you call Hicks an old goat to his face."

"Did he give us away? Did Wyatt question him?"

"If you haven't realized this yet," Dan said, "Wyatt is kind of in the middle of a big race. I hardly think he gave much thought to Hicks being here."

Sam could accept that logic. "Good," he said. "That's good. Because I want to surprise him."

"I'm aware," Dan said.

"How much longer, do you think?"

"Two minutes."

"Really?"

Dan turned toward Sam, and though his eyes were hidden behind his own shades, Sam knew he was scowling. "How the hell do I know?"

Sam decided to just train his eyes on the finish line. It was genuinely inspiring to see so many people crossing the line, pain and relief and joy on their faces. It was a crazy accomplishment, Sam thought. He'd never be able to run that far, and he was in awe of anyone with the discipline to do so.

The finish line was on a straight stretch, so the spectators could see the runners coming for the last fourth of a mile or so. In the distance, Sam thought he caught a glimpse of a familiar lean frame. "Is that him?" He pointed, which was completely unhelpful.

Dan didn't respond at first, but he was looking at the route intently. "I think so," he said.

A few moments later, Sam was certain. He saw a dark man bun and bright blue running shoes and knew it was his man. Wyatt was striding confidently, at a solid pace, looking like he wasn't tired in the least. Sam's stomach flipped and his heart thudded, kicking up several notches at the sight of Wyatt. Without thinking, Sam started toward the finish line, making his way closer and closer, squeezing past other spectators. Dan grabbed his arm and halted him after a few steps. "Don't get too far ahead of me," he warned.

Sam didn't take his eyes off Wyatt. His legs flexed as he ran, and his movements were mesmerizingly elegant for having just run a ridiculous distance. Sam was struck dumb by him. He was amazing. Wyatt didn't seem to notice him, and he supposed that could be due to the fact Wyatt was coming to the end of thirteen miles of running and was overwhelmed and exhausted, though he didn't look it at all, if you asked Sam. Sam had been pretty careful about keeping his ball cap low over his eyes, and he wore dark glasses. He'd dressed as nondescript as possible, and so far, no one in the crowd had recognized him, which was the point. However, as Wyatt neared, he really needed him to know he was there cheering him on. With each stride Wyatt made nearer, Sam itched to shed his disguise and jump up and down, screaming Wyatt's name. He needed Wyatt to see him there.

"Be cool," Dan said, his voice stern. It was almost like the big guy could read Sam's mind; he knew him too well.

Sam's heart pounded faster and harder each second as Wyatt neared the finish line. Sam watched him finishing strong, his strides even and steady, his arms pumping along as he propelled himself forward with incredible grace. He was only a few yards from the finish line, and Sam couldn't help himself. He took his sunglasses off, ripped off his cap, and he handed them to Dan as he dashed off toward the barricade near the finish line. A stunned Dan was hollering behind him. "Hey! Stop!"

Sam ignored him, reaching the barrier and waving his arms over his head, yelling, "Wyatt! Wyatt! Way to go!" He was hopping up and down, his red hair flopping all over the place, and as Wyatt crossed the finish line, Sam felt tears sting his eyes. He'd never felt so proud of someone. The spectators at the finish line applauded for Wyatt and everyone else completing the race near him. There were cheers and high fives and hugs, and through tear-blurred eyes, Sam found Wyatt. "Wyatt," he called again, waving like a loon. Wyatt saw him then, and his face lit up. Sam charged him, tackling Wyatt into a bear hug. Sam felt Wyatt's sweat-soaked back under his palms as Wyatt's shaking arms wrapped around Sam. "You're such a badass!

I'm so freaking proud of you," Sam said into the side of Wyatt's face, Sam not caring one bit about Wyatt's damp hair against his own temple. He squeezed him tightly, hoping to convey all the elation, joy, and pride he felt in that moment with the ferocity of his embrace.

"You came," Wyatt said, and Sam could hear the emotion in his voice, as well. Wyatt wasn't in a hurry to let him go, and Sam's chest clenched with the overwhelming emotion of having him in his arms again, sharing this special moment with him. That Wyatt wanted to share it with him meant everything.

"I wouldn't have missed it," Sam said, laughing and crying and clinging to his man.

"Sorry to interrupt," Dan's gruff voice cut into their moment. "But you have a bit of an audience here, guys."

Sam and Wyatt didn't care. Hicks and Wilkinson had appeared, and the three bodyguards had formed a bit of a perimeter around Wyatt and Sam, keeping the onlookers back, though they couldn't stop their cell phone cameras.

"This is going to be all over social media," Dan said, again attempting to break Sam and Wyatt out of their reunion daze and come back to reality. "We're going to have to get you out of here." Sam felt a big hand gently tap his shoulder, and he knew Dan was genuinely concerned about their safety.

"Okay," Sam said as he pulled back from Wyatt just enough to look him in the eye. "We can go after one more thing," Sam said, speaking to Dan, though his eyes were on Wyatt.

"What?" Dan asked.

"This," Sam said, reaching up to cup Wyatt's face. "I love you, Wyatt Price. And I will be here for you forever. No matter what." He leaned in and kissed Wyatt on the lips, a firm and promising press of his lips, punctuating the promise he'd just made.

Sam was vaguely aware of the whoops and cheers of the spectators who had shifted their attention from the finishing line of the race and turned their focus to Sam and Wyatt's reunion. He didn't care. He was confident that Dan and the other security officers could keep them safe, especially with the additional law enforcement presence at the race. Still, Sam didn't dare take chances with Wyatt's safety, so he took Wyatt's hand and let Dan, Hicks, and Wilkinson usher them toward their vehicles.

When they reached the spot security had parked the SUVs, Bowen and Clark were waiting there, and they both heartily congratulated Wyatt, Bowen pulling him in for a hug and Clark slapping his back and ruffling his hair. Bowen wrapped an insulated blanket around Wyatt's shoulders and a bottle of water. It took a few minutes for Wyatt's body to come down from the run, and the exhaustion was starting to sink in. "Let's get you in a vehicle," Sam said, and they divided up into the SUVs, Sam and Wyatt getting into the back of the one driven by Danson, Clark and Bowen hopping in with Wilkinson and Hicks. In the quiet and privacy of the SUV's back seat, Sam and Wyatt sat as close to one another as possible, not taking their eyes or hands off one another, their fingers twined together, resting on Sam's thigh. They didn't speak, perhaps because they were both so overwhelmed with the intensity of the moment, but they grinned at one another and randomly burst out in mirthful giggles as Dan maneuvered them out of the race-day traffic.

From the front seat, Dan looked back at them in the rearview mirror and grumbled a "congratulations."

"Thanks, Danson," Wyatt said, though Dan's eyes met Sam's, and Sam saw a small quirk of Dan's lips that might have qualified as a smile for Dan. Sam was fairly certain the well wishes were as much for Sam as they were for Wyatt completing his race. And truth be told, Sam genuinely felt like the biggest winner in the world. He lifted their joined hands, and Sam kissed the back of Wyatt's hand.

"I love you too," Wyatt whispered. "Thank you for being here."

"I'll be anywhere you want me to be," Sam whispered back. "Anywhere. Always."

They nuzzled their noses together and kissed softly.

"You stink, though," Sam said softly in Wyatt's ear.

Wyatt drew back and gave him a death glare that Sam thought looked more adorable than intimidating, though he would never tell that to Wyatt.

"But I still love your stinky face," Sam said, grinning at Wyatt until Wyatt broke and his scowl turned into a broad, unrestrained smile.

\* \* \*

It was a bit like déjà vu when Dan and Sam pulled out of Sam's apartment complex and headed out into the neighborhood. "Uh, Dan-o?"

"What?" Dan sounded dubious already, and Sam had barely spoken. The man knew Sam far, far too well.

"We need to make a quick detour," Sam said.

"We don't have time for detours," Dan said.

"Actually, we do," Sam said. "I told you I had a 9:00 a.m. call time, but it's really 10:30."

Dan shot daggers at Sam, who flashed his 800,000-dollar-an-episode grin. "Sorry, not sorry," he said. "So, we have plenty of time to swing by the cafe." Dan grumbled but took a left in the direction of the cafe. "That was easier

209

than I thought," Sam said. "You're getting soft in your old age, Big D." Dan didn't respond, and Sam pushed his luck. There were few things he loved more than getting Dan's goat. "It wouldn't have anything to do with Monty, would it?"

"No," Dan said quickly. Too quickly.

Sam cackled. Monty was the new doorman at the cafe. Sure, it was not customary to have a doorman at a cafe, but ever since Sam and Wyatt's public lovefest at the half-marathon, there was nearly always a handful of Sam's fans loitering around the cafe to catch a glimpse of Wyatt. Some paparazzi also camped out across the street from the cafe for the first week or so following the breaking news of Sam Deerwood's romance with the raven-haired cafe employee, but they'd eventually moved on to shinier, higher-drama celebrities. But Sam and Bowen had both agreed they'd feel better having a beefy don't-fuck-with-Wyatt presence at the cafe when Wyatt was there, so while Sam and Wyatt were both adamant that a full-time security guard, especially one the caliber of Wilkinson, was overkill, they'd agreed to compromise by hiring Monty—Weston Montgomery—as a doorman for any fans that crossed the line. Essentially, he was a bouncer for anyone who was at the cafe to hassle Wyatt rather than order lattes. Initially, Dan had balked at the idea because Monty wasn't an "official" security guard with training like his. But his charisma and sheer bulk made him a quick favorite among the staff and clientele alike. And, even begrudgingly, Dan seemed to take a shine to him, and that was endlessly amusing for Sam.

When they reached the cafe's entrance, Monty and Sam exchanged an elaborate handshake that involved many intricate steps that Dan rolled his eyes about every time they performed it. "Weston," Dan said curtly as he passed, up-nodding at him ever so slightly.

"Danson," Monty said with a wide grin. "Good to see you as always." Dan grunted something, and Sam delighted at what he was certain was a flush on the big guy's cheeks.

The cafe was mostly empty, aside from a couple of women in their mid-sixties sipping coffees at a corner table. No one was behind the counter, and Sam moseyed over, leaning against it casually. Soon, the swinging door from the kitchen flung open, and Wyatt emerged with two large boxes of baked goods in his arms, Bowen following him with a matching pair of his own. When Wyatt saw Sam, he sat his boxes down and leaned over the counter to kiss Sam hello.

"I missed you," Sam murmured against Wyatt's lips.

Wyatt gave Sam three quick pecks before pulling away. "It's been four hours, babe," Wyatt said.

"I know," Sam said. "Way too long."

They'd been spending every night together, but Wyatt often had to sneak out of Sam's place in the wee hours of the morning to do the cafe's bakery run and all his opening duties.

The bell over the door chimed, and two teenage girls walked in. Sam could hear Monty question them. "Shouldn't you two be in school?"

They giggled and batted their lashes at Monty, as most people did. Monty was definitely a gorgeous man. "No school today," they said. "End of the term."

Monty let them pass because they'd adopted an innocent-until-proven-crazy fangirl policy, though he tended to be wary of anyone under the age of twenty who entered the cafe. Or their mothers. As the girls neared the counter to order, Sam ducked out of the way, pretending to be very interested in the various business cards and flyers tacked up on the bulletin board above the cart with creams and sugars.

Bowen was just about done putting the new baked goods into the glass case beside the register, so Wyatt was the one to wait on the customers. "What can I get you?" Wyatt's voice was cheerful, and Sam always marveled at how comfortable Wyatt seemed when he was working with customers. Wyatt truly never gave himself enough credit for how capable he was of getting out of his shell when need be.

"Oh," the first girl said. "I'll have a caramel latte with an extra shot and whipped cream, please."

Wyatt took a cup and wrote some form of shorthand that apparently indicated all of that. The next girl waited until Wyatt looked up at her. "Just a selfie for me, please." She smiled, all false lashes and too much lipstick.

"Uh..." Wyatt didn't seem to understand, and his eyes flicked over to where Sam was standing. Dan was lingering nearby, and he definitely stood at attention at the mention of a selfie. "I don't know what you mean..."

The girl rolled her eyes. "I'm a big fan," she said. "Can I just get one selfie? For my running club?"

Sam watched out of the corner of his eye, loving how adorable Wyatt looked with the blush on his cheeks. His life had definitely changed since he and Sam had come out publicly with their relationship, but it wasn't in the way they'd expected. Lots of the social media buzz had been about "Sam Deerwood's hot runner boyfriend" or "'It' couple Sam and Wyatt spotted jogging in the park," etc. Most of the publicity had been positive, supportive, and very favorable about Wyatt and Sam's relationship. There were, of course, a few assholes, but that was unavoidable in any situation. What was most surprising to them all, Wyatt especially, was how many fans Wyatt had. Sam couldn't blame them, though. He was beautiful and wonderful and amazing. Of course Sam's fans fell in love with him.

Wyatt was still looking at the girl with confusion when she explained. "My friends and I just love you. We signed up for the Humane Society 5K because of you, you know."

Sam smiled and turned the corner, approaching the girls. "I'll take the photo for you if you both want to get in the picture," he offered. They gawped at Sam for a second before the girl who'd asked for the selfie handed him her phone. "Come on, babe," Sam said, motioning for Wyatt to come out from around the corner.

"I'll make that drink," Bowen offered, winking at Sam as he pushed Wyatt toward them.

"Stand together," Sam said, and the teens flanked Wyatt, each wrapping an arm around him. "Say 'running shorts,'" Sam said. The girls did. Wyatt gave a confused half smile. Sam handed the phone back, Bowen placed the first girl's drink on the counter, and they left.

"What's it like playing second fiddle to your man?" Bowen asked Sam.

"I get it," Sam said. He smiled at Wyatt. "What's not to love?"

# Epilogue

## Wyatt

"**D**id they practice actual choreography for a karaoke performance? What the hell?" Sam looked equal parts disbelieving and enraged as he watched his sister, Tyson, and Harlow shimmy and twirl in front of Bowen and Clark's massive living room window. It was dark out, so the light of the moon and the distant twinkle of homes in the Hollywood Hills sparkled against the black sky, serving as the perfect backdrop to the undeniably entertaining rendition of "Bang Bang."

"They are pretty good, though," Wyatt said, hoping to get a further rise out of Sam. Teasing his boyfriend was one of his favorite pastimes, after all. "I think Harlow is a killer Ariana."

Sam's eyes widened and his head whipped to face Wyatt, incredulous. "Well Mara is certainly no Jessie J. I mean, seriously." Sam gestured toward the front of the room where his sister was performing enthusiastic, if off-key vocal runs. If Wyatt was honest, Mara wasn't great. But Tyson and Harlow were amazing, and they more than made up for her lack of polish.

"You'll just have to show 'em how it's really done, babe." Wyatt squeezed Sam's knee, smiling sweetly.

Sam seemed to consider that. "Well, the song I was planning to do won't cut it now," Sam said, like he was plotting his revenge as they spoke. "I'm going to need to up my game. How can I honestly compete with a trio, though...?" He trailed off, his brows knitting together as he plotted.

"You got this," Wyatt said. "I have faith in you." Sam eyed him in a manner that made Wyatt's brows raise. Sam looked to be scheming, and when Sam was scheming, Wyatt knew that nothing good would come of it. At least nothing Wyatt would approve of.

"I certainly do have this," Sam said, his lips curling into a Cheshire Cat smile. "We've got this," he amended, taking Wyatt's hand as Mara and Co. finished up their song. Sam stood and tugged Wyatt to his feet along with him.

"What are you doing?" Wyatt felt a surge of panic hit his gut as Sam dragged him to the front of the crowded living room. The space was packed with their family— Clark and Bowen, Matt and Jasper, Mara, Tyson, and Harlow, sans Milo, who was with Harlow's mom for the evening. Danson and Monty also hung back by the kitchen island. Danson was practically family at this point, and Monty had become a welcome addition to the crew, not only as a trusted employee but as a close friend to Matt and Jasper. Wyatt was as comfortable with this crew of people as he was with any group. But that didn't mean he liked being the center of attention.

"You're singing with me," Sam said. "I need to pull out all the stops, and a duet is the only way." Wyatt tried to root his feet in place, but Sam continued to tug him forward. Their family cheered as Sam and his reluctant partner reached the front of the room. Sam turned to Wyatt, gripping both his hands, and he whispered, "You don't have to. But if there is any part of you that is okay with trying this for me, I will love you forever."

"You will love me forever anyway," Wyatt said.

"True." Sam's eyes glinted and his red hair fell over his forehead in an adorable mess that still never failed to melt Wyatt's heart. He thought about how much he loved this man, and how far they'd come together. Wyatt was more and more used to being in the proverbial spotlight since they'd come out as a couple. But their strategy of not hiding anything and just going about their normal, mundane, boring old business seemed to keep the fans and paparazzi at bay. Sure, they would still get stopped if they went out in public, but it wasn't nearly the issue Sam and his security team had feared it might be. And, truth be told, once fans knew Sam was definitely off the market, they'd been very supportive of their relationship. It was sweet, really. Aside from the people that insisted on making Wyatt into a quasi celebrity among the LA runner's circuit. But even that had become easier for Wyatt as time went on. Sam had worked exceedingly hard to manage his fame in a way that wouldn't be too disruptive to Wyatt and their life together. And for that, Wyatt would be forever grateful. And the least he could do was make some compromises for Sam in return. Even if they made Wyatt feel light-headed and want to puke a bit.

"What song?" Wyatt asked begrudgingly. Sam's face absolutely lit up, and while Wyatt knew he'd come to regret this in short order, when it truly came down to it, there was nothing he could deny Sam. There never had been.

"Really? You'll sing with me?" Sam was practically bouncing up and down with elation.

"I'll stand there and try to get the words right while you do your thing. But I can't promise I'll be any good at it."

"Oh, you'll be terrible." Sam grinned so wide his eyes nearly closed with it. "But it'll be fabulous." He smacked a quick kiss on Wyatt's lips and knelt at the iPad where the karaoke app was pulled up. "How about...'Baby Got Back'?"

"No," Wyatt said quickly and firmly.

Everyone laughed, and Sam tapped around, then stood, grabbing the mic and holding it between him and Wyatt.

"What did you choose?" Wyatt asked, wincing when he realized he'd spoken loudly into the mic.

"Do you trust me?" Sam held his gaze.

"Unfortunately, yes," Wyatt said. "I trust you."

The music started up, a familiar tune that Wyatt recognized immediately. Sam had played the song on his guitar a thousand times while they'd lounged around the apartment on a lazy Sunday or while they spent a Friday night in. It was one of Wyatt's favorites—a James Bay and Julia Michaels duet—and he couldn't help but smile. The words appeared on the iPad screen, and Wyatt nudged Sam with his shoulder affectionately, and Sam winked at him. They didn't need to sort out who would be taking which part. Wyatt knew. And when Sam started the first verse of "Peer Pressure," the nerves dissolved, and Wyatt felt at home. Because he was.

# Acknowledgments

This book has been a whole journey. For Sam and Wyatt, certainly, but for me, too. This series has been life-changing for me. It was where I started out, and it is something I am immensely proud of.

It has been challenging to get this book out into the world. I wanted to do the characters justice, and I had a lot of struggles. But the end result is something I couldn't be happier with, and that is due, in large part, to the support system that I have.

My kids, who are endlessly proud of me, give me so much motivation. So I'm thankful for them. (They aren't reading this, but they deserve a mention.)

Thank you, Garry Michael, my partner in bookish crime, for always having my back, hyping me up, and never letting me give up on anything.

A huge thank you to Michaela Cole, who gets me. You are the person I turn to when I have the crazy thoughts that either require talking off the ledge or an enthusiastic urging to roll with the chaos. You are the best.

Thank you to Matthew Dante, Michael Robert, Harper Robson, L.D. Blakeley, Duckie Mack, Kota Quinn, and S.M. Landon, who are all fantastic colleagues and friends. Thanks for putting up with me.

To the readers and social media family that has embraced me through the ups and downs, I love and appreciate all of you so much! You know who you are. Thank you.

Lastly, a HUGE thank-you to everyone who has supported me on Patreon. I am so, so grateful for you!

# About the Author

Jeris Jean is the author of the Hollywood Hopefuls and Coleridge Cliffs series. Jeris loves reading in general, but mm romance is her true passion. She puts her English Lit degree and rabid consumption of reading material to work to bring readers all the sweet and sexy and swoony feels. Jeris has more story ideas than time on earth to write them all, but she hopes to bring as many as she can to life.

Jeris loves cats, puzzles, knitting, and full sugar Coca-Cola. She lives in a delightful little suburb of Minneapolis/St. Paul with her family and cat, Fluffy Cat Love, and she couldn't love the Twin Cities more.

She is a night owl, always tired, always reading, and always jotting down ideas in one of many notebooks full of messy, colorful scrawl any time inspiration strikes.

Get exclusive early access to Jeris's new WIPs, merch, and bonus content by joining Jeris's Patreon today: https://www.patreon.com/jerisjean

# Also by Jeris Jean

## *Coleridge Cliffs Series*

Romantic Hero

Historic Event

Classic Dilemma

## *Hollywood Hopefuls Series*

Running Lines

Drawing Lines

Crossing Lines

Opening Lines

Finishing Lines

Cruising: An M/M Anthology

Ingram Content Group UK Ltd.
Milton Keynes UK
UKHW010631220523
422140UK00001B/18

9 798223 164388